TRIXIE BELDEN®

The TRIXIE BELDEN Series

1 The Secret of the Mansion
2 The Red Trailer Mystery
3 The Gatehouse Mystery
4 The Mysterious Visitor
5 The Mystery Off Glen Road
6 The Mystery in Arizona
7 The Mysterious Code
8 The Black Jacket Mystery
9 The Happy Valley Mystery
10 The Marshland Mystery
11 The Mystery at Bob-White Cave
12 The Mystery of the Blinking Eye
13 The Mystery on Cobbett's Island
14 The Mystery of the Emeralds
15 The Mystery on the Mississippi
16 The Mystery of the Missing Heiress
17 The Mystery of the Uninvited Guest
18 The Mystery of the Phantom Grasshopper
19 The Secret of the Unseen Treasure
20 The Mystery Off Old Telegraph Road
21 The Mystery of the Castaway Children
22 The Mystery at Mead's Mountain
23 The Mystery of the Queen's Necklace
24 The Mystery at Saratoga
25 The Sasquatch Mystery
26 The Mystery of the Headless Horseman
27 The Mystery of the Ghostly Galleon
28 The Hudson River Mystery
29 The Mystery of the Velvet Gown
30 The Mystery of the Midnight Marauder
31 The Mystery at Maypenny's
32 The Mystery of the Whispering Witch
33 The Mystery of the Vanishing Victim
34 The Mystery of the Missing Millionaire
35 The Mystery of the Memorial Day Fire
36 The Mystery of the Antique Doll

TRIXIE BELDEN®

THE MYSTERY OF THE OF THE ANTIQUE DOLL

By Kathryn Kenny

Black-and-white illustrations by Jim Spence

A GOLDEN BOOK • NEW YORK

Western Publishing Company, Inc., Racine, Wisconsin 53404

Contents

1 The Doctor's Request   9
2 Trixie and Honey Help Out   23
3 The Curious Antique Shop   37
4 Trixie Investigates   50
5 An Unusual Favor   62
6 The Parisian Doll   77
7 A Suspicious Stranger   95
8 Wrongly Accused   107
9 The Clue in the Dress   122
10 Caught!   134
11 Trixie's Plan   147
12 No Escape   158
13 The Rescuers   170
14 The Sergeant's Commendation   181

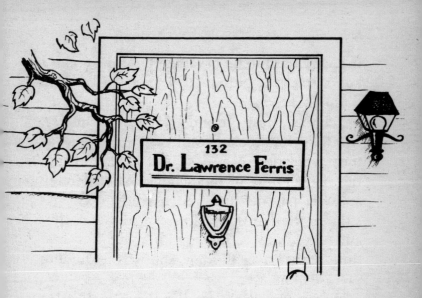

1 * The Doctor's Request

"OH, NOT AGAIN!" yelped fourteen-year-old Trixie Belden, as her books went crashing to the stairs. The flow of students leaving Sleepyside Junior-Senior High School stopped for barely a minute as Trixie tried to collect the scattered papers from her loose-leaf notebook. "That's the second time today!"

Irritably, Trixie pushed a short lock of sandy-blonde hair out of her eyes. She put the last book on the pile, and said, "I'm trying very hard to be organized, but how can I keep track of things if I constantly drop them?"

Trixie's best friend, Honey Wheeler, laughed. She gazed fondly at her friend as they went down the last few steps and into the main lobby of the school. When Honey and her parents had first moved to Sleepy-side-on-the-Hudson, Honey had been thin and shy. Now, after spending all her free time with Trixie Belden, she was a glowing picture of health.

Honey was slightly taller than Trixie. Her shoulder-length, honey-blonde hair was always combed, and her school books were always organized. Neatness was one of the things she'd learned in the boarding schools she'd gone to before moving to Sleepyside. Together, Trixie and Honey had solved many mysteries, and they planned to open the Belden-Wheeler Detective Agency someday. But first they had a few things to take care of, such as getting out the door with all their belongings intact.

As they walked out of school into the late afternoon sunshine, Trixie squinted and raised her hand to shade her eyes.

"There you are!" came a slightly mocking voice from behind them. "Procrastinating in the halls is hardly a sign of mental acuity!"

"Oh, Mart," Trixie said, with a grin. "Is Moms waiting for us? I was just looking for the car." Mart was Trixie's "almost twin" brother. They were eleven months apart and, even though Mart was older, people often mistook them for twins.

"Why is Moms picking you up?" Mart asked, a look of surprise on his face. "Aren't you two going to the staff meeting of the newspaper? It's this afternoon, you know."

"I know," Trixie answered, "but we're going with Moms to see Dr. Ferris. Bobby has to have his checkup. He said he wouldn't go unless Honey and I came, too."

"Would you explain to the others why we can't make it?" Honey said sweetly. "And let us know if we have any assignments for the next issue."

"Your wish is my command," Mart said, bowing low and making a sweeping motion with his arm. "Now that you mention it, I do remember something about a visit to the good Dr. Ferris being bruited about at the breakfast table this morning."

Mart gave Trixie an affectionate pat on the head—which he knew she hated—and disappeared into the school building. The late fall sun had sunk even lower, and Trixie again tried to find the Belden station wagon among the cars and buses parked in front of the school.

"There they are!" Honey shouted suddenly, and the girls dashed over to the car.

Helen Belden waved and smiled as she saw them approach. Then she turned to six-year-old Bobby Belden who was sitting in the back seat. His chubby, angelic face had a very gloomy expression on it. He didn't even perk up when Honey stuck her head in the window to plant a kiss on his mop of blond curls.

"I'm glad you took so long," Bobby said, thrusting out his lower lip. "Now maybe I missed my appointment with the doctor."

"Not quite," Mrs. Belden said, with a wink. "We still have plenty of time. Hop in, girls."

Trixie and Honey settled themselves in the back seat on either side of the grumpy little boy. Mrs. Belden started the engine, but before she could pull away from the crowded curb, the car was suddenly surrounded by three students wearing matching red jackets. Cross-stitched on the back of each jacket were the letters B.W.G.

"Oh no," Helen Belden moaned. "What next!"

She smiled affectionately at the sight of her handsome, seventeen-year-old son Brian who was with two of his friends—Diana Lynch and Jim Frayne.

Jim's full name was James Winthrop Frayne III. When his eccentric uncle died a few years before, he left Jim a half-million dollars in trust. But Jim was then living with his cruel stepfather, Jonesy, who wanted to steal Jim's inheritance. Trixie had helped Jim get away from Jonesy. Then Honey's parents adopted Jim, and now Jim was saving his inheritance to open a school for homeless boys.

"We just wanted to give Bobby a special Bob-White send-off, and tell him that he has to try and be very, very good at Dr. Ferris's office," Brian said cheerfully. He reached in the window and tousled Bobby's hair.

"Now remember, there's nothing to be afraid of," Jim said. "Dr. Ferris is the one who keeps us well, and helps us get better if we get sick."

"That's right," Di chimed in. Diana Lynch, who preferred to be called Di, was known as the prettiest girl in school. She had shiny black hair, and her violet eyes were fringed with long, black lashes. When her family had been poor, they'd lived in a small apartment on Main Street. However, after her father became rich, they moved to a big estate on Glen Road. The Lynch estate was not far from the Manor House where the Wheelers lived or from the Belden family's home, Crabapple Farm.

The young people were all members of a club called the Bob-Whites of the Glen, or B.W.G.'s for short. They formed the semisecret club both to have fun and to help others. There were seven members altogether: Trixie, Mart, and Brian Belden; Honey Wheeler and her adopted brother, Jim Frayne; Di Lynch; and Dan Mangan. Dan had lived in New York City, but now went to Sleepyside Junior-Senior High School. The nephew of Bill Regan, the Wheelers' groom, Dan had come to live in Sleepyside and work with Mr. Maypenny, the Wheelers' gamekeeper.

All the Bob-Whites had agreed that other people could know about their club, but not about the good deeds they did. The one absolute rule of the club was that the dues they paid had to be earned through their own work. It wasn't always easy, but they managed.

"If you children don't let me pull away from this curb," Mrs. Belden said, "there won't be any reason to give Bobby a send-off. At this rate we'll be late and, what's more, you'll miss your school bus and have to walk home. Now get along with you."

She waved her hand at them as if she were shooing chickens, and then drove the car out onto the road heading south to the doctor's office. In a few minutes, they arrived, pulled into a parking space, and piled out of the car. Bobby hung back, but before he could say a word, Honey scooped him up into her arms and kissed him on the side of his neck. He giggled and squirmed as Honey carried him up the steps.

"Kissing tickles!" he shrieked as they stepped into the waiting room.

"Good," Honey said. "At least you're laughing, right?"

Dr. Ferris poked his head out of the examination room when he heard the door-chime.

"You'd make a good doctor, Miss Wheeler," he said as he watched Honey play with Bobby Belden. "You know how to keep the patients laughing, and that's almost as important as the rest of the work doctors do!"

"Oh, Doctor Ferris," Honey said. "That's kind of you to say, but I truly doubt it."

"Master Bobby Belden," Dr. Ferris said loudly, "could that be you? Step right this way. Why, you seem to have grown the unbelievable amount of three feet in six months! We'd better measure you. It could be that I'm looking at the fastest-growing boy in the United States!"

Bobby reluctantly slid off his chair, and, holding Honey's hand tightly, he followed his mother and big sister into the examination room.

Bobby was a very "brave boy" while the doctor examined him. When the checkup was over, Bobby heaved a gigantic sigh of relief and announced that he didn't need to hold Honey's hand anymore.

Only then did Dr. Ferris turn his attention away from his little patient, and address the two girls.

"You know, girls," he said, looking at them over the tops of his bifocals, "I have a patient who needs a little help and I was hoping you two could lend a hand."

He glanced briefly at Mrs. Belden and then continued.

"Mrs. De Keyser, who lives about a mile away from you on Glen Road, slipped and broke her arm the other day. For the next couple of weeks she's going to have a hard time doing some chores. She doesn't need to hire a private nurse—her condition isn't that bad—but she needs a little light work done for her. Do you think you two could handle it?"

"Of course," Trixie burst out. "It wouldn't be any problem at all!"

"Think before you make any promises," Mrs. Belden said, eyeing her enthusiastic daughter. "Remember, you're supposed to be studying for the Eastern Regional Spelling Contest, and you have homework."

"Gleeps, Moms, I know all that," Trixie said. "But I always have some time to help someone out, don't I?"

"Yes, I suppose you always do," Mrs. Belden said with a proud smile.

"If we both help, it'll be easy," Honey offered. "We can get the school bus driver to let us off at Mrs. De Keyser's house after school."

"And we were going to study for the spelling contest together anyway," Trixie said. "We can test each other while we work. So this won't interfere at all."

"I knew I could count on you girls," Dr. Ferris said. He finished jotting down a few notes on Bobby's record, and then stood up.

"Isn't Mrs. De Keyser the one who lives next to the new antique store that just opened on Glen Road?" Trixie asked, as she helped Bobby put on his coat. "We always see it as we go by on the school bus. We've been wanting to stop in and have a look."

"That's her," Dr. Ferris replied. "The store is called The Antique Barn, I believe, and it's right next door to Mrs. De Keyser's house."

"Well, now we'll get a chance to look at all the antiques," Honey said hopefully. "Should we stop by Mrs. De Keyser's house this afternoon, or do you think it can wait until tomorrow?"

"Tomorrow will be just fine. I'll tell her to

expect you," Dr. Ferris said, ushering them out the door. "And, Bobby, I want you to keep right on eating all that good food your mother makes for you, and grow up big and strong."

"Like your sister, right?" Trixie giggled and made a small muscle in her arm.

"Superman!" Bobby yelled, as he jumped down the three steps of the doctor's office and ran ahead to the car.

Trixie and Honey climbed in after him, and Mrs. Belden backed out of the parking lot. She drove back toward town, and soon they came to Main Street.

"I have to stop at the market before we go home," she said. "I'm out of onions. I won't be long, so why don't you three just stay in the car and wait for me?"

But as she was about to pull the car into the one empty space in front of the little grocery store, another car shot in front of her and pulled into the spot. Helen Belden jammed on the brakes and just managed to avoid hitting the other car broadside.

"Well, of all the nerve," she said, surprised at the other driver's behavior. "Oh, well, I guess I'll just go into that spot across the street."

"Who was it, Moms?" Trixie asked.

"I'm not sure," her mother answered. "But it doesn't matter. I'll be right back, kids."

While they waited in the car, Bobby played the game he loved most when he was with his older brothers. Trixie was not good at the game, but she agreed to play because Bobby had been such a good boy.

"That's a Ford!" Bobby yelled as he watched a car go by. "And that's a Bee-yoo-ick!"

"You're absolutely right," Honey said. She winked at Trixie, and leaned over to whisper in Bobby's ear.

"Bobby, when you play this game with us, you're always right. Do you know why?"

"Yes," Bobby said firmly. "Because you don't know the names of any of the cars and I know all of them, that's why."

"That's right," Honey said. "But then how do we know when you've made a mistake?"

"I never make a mistake," Bobby said, smiling happily.

"Hey," Trixie said, tapping Honey on the

arm. "Take a look at that car—the one that cut Moms off."

She pointed to the sleek maroon foreign sedan that had cut off Mrs. Belden. It was still parked across the street.

"That's a Mercedes-Benz! Neat-o," Bobby said, trying to purse his mouth into a whistle. A lot of air came out, but no whistle.

Just then, Mrs. Belden came out of the store with her package. She was walking behind a man with his hat pulled down low over his eyes. The collar of his camel's hair coat was turned up. He hurriedly got into the Mercedes-Benz, and started to back out into the oncoming traffic. Horns honked loudly.

Mrs. Belden got behind the wheel of the station wagon. "Well, he's certainly in a big rush," she said. Her exasperation was evident in the tone of her voice. "He pushed ahead of me at the check-out counter."

"Who is that?" asked Trixie. "Does he live in Sleepyside?"

"The cashier said he's the man who just opened The Antique Barn next to Mrs. De Keyser's house," Mrs. Belden said, collecting herself.

"Well, he has a very nice car," Trixie said, as she watched it drive off into the early dusk. "Looks to me as if a person could make an awful lot of money in the antique business, doesn't it?"

"What?" asked Honey. She had not been paying attention.

"Maybe we ought to consider an annual antique fair to raise money for the Bob-Whites and for UNICEF," said Trixie. "We did pretty well the last time we tried it."

Trixie was thinking about the time the Bob-Whites held a fair not only to raise money for UNICEF, but also to prove to the principal of their school and the members of the school board that they weren't a "bad" gang. In the course of collecting antiques for the show, they had discovered a mysterious code and a mystery to solve.

"We made money, Trixie, but not enough to buy a car like that," Honey answered, with a laugh. "A Mercedes-Benz costs thousands and thousands of dollars!"

"You know," Trixie said thoughtfully, "you're right. I'm willing to bet there's something funny about that man—and his antique business, too."

2 * Trixie and Honey Help Out

"SCURRILOUS," Mart said, grinning devilishly. He glanced briefly at the paper in his hand, and then looked at Trixie expectantly.

"Er, s-c-u-r-r-i-l—is it one *l* or two?" asked Trixie, as she stumbled onto the school bus and got a seat near the back.

"One," Mart said, sliding in behind her. "Start from the beginning again."

"Oh, all right. S-c-u-r-r-i-l-o-u-s!" Trixie said.

Honey, who was sitting next to Trixie,

pulled out the word list to check the correct
spelling. Both of them were finalists in the
local spelling contest. They were studying
hard for the Eastern Regional Spelling Contest that would be held in New York City
in two weeks. The winner of the Eastern
Regional would get a chance at the national
competition in Washington, D.C.

"Fish," Mart said, with a pompous expression on his face.

"Fish?" Trixie said. "Fish isn't on that
list!"

"So what? I'm the one who's testing you,"
Mart said, "so you have to spell the words I
give you. Now, spell fish!"

"F-i-s-h!" Trixie shouted.

"Wrong," Mart said, with a haughty sniff.
"It's g-h-o-t-i."

"It is not!" Trixie wailed. "And you're
wasting my time with all this."

"Now wait a minute," Mart said. "This is
an example of how ridiculous spelling in the
English language can be. See, *gh* is the *f*
sound in *rough*; *o* is the *i* sound in *women*; *ti*
is the *sh* sound in *motion*. So—g-h-o-t-i!
Fish!"

"If you're so smart, Mart Belden," Trixie

snapped, "why didn't you win the spelling contest, huh?"

Mart blushed furiously and looked at the floor. Although he was the smartest of all the Beldens, Mart had a lot of trouble with spelling.

"I only understand things that have intrinsically logical rules," Mart snapped back peevishly. "And spelling is based on centuries of erroneous whims, dubious derivations, and illogical usage. It is, consequently, beneath my contempt!"

"Only someone who can't spell would say something like that," Trixie began. But when she saw her brother's embarrassment she felt bad.

"Oh, I'm sorry, Mart. Come on, ask me another one!"

"How about fluorescence?" Mart said, regaining his usual superior attitude.

"Oh goodness," Trixie said, with a sigh. "Are you sure that's one of the words?"

"Yup," Mart said efficiently. "Hurry up. You haven't got all day, you know."

"Ugh! F-l-u-o-r-e-s—um—c-e-n-c-e!"

"Perfect, little sister. Your mnemonics are improving!"

"Her what?" Honey said as the bus turned a corner.

"Mnemonics is the art of developing the memory," Mart explained. "And furthermore—"

"Gleeps!" Trixie yelled, leaping to her feet in the lurching bus. "Speaking of memory, Honey, we're getting off now. Don't you remember? We're stopping to help Mrs. De Keyser."

Trixie dashed to the front of the bus. She bent down and explained the unexpected stop to the bus driver, who nodded. The bus wheezed to a halt in front of a trim little white house, and Honey and Trixie clattered down the steps. They waved to Mart as the bus pulled away from them.

Trixie shivered as she zipped up her jacket.

"It might be time to start wearing a sweater under this. I can't believe that winter will soon be here. Only last week it was Halloween!"

Honey pulled her jacket closed, and zipped up too. They were standing on the shoulder of Glen Road between Mrs. De

Keyser's house and a beautifully restored barn with a brand-new sign hanging over the door. Dark blue letters outlined in gold said THE ANTIQUE BARN.

"I like the sign," Trixie said, glancing up appraisingly. "It looks old-fashioned and nice, doesn't it?"

"Yes, it does," Honey agreed. "But Mrs. De Keyser is expecting us, so we'd better go in and see what has to be done."

The two girls went up the flagstone walk, and climbed the steps of the wide porch. The front door had a lovely semicircular stained-glass window set near the top. Trixie raised the lion-head knocker and rapped sharply.

A few moments later, they heard the shuffling noise that slippers make when they're finally broken in and comfortable. The door swung open, and a rosy-cheeked little woman stood on the other side, smiling at them. Her arm was in a cast and she wore a colorful, Chinese-silk scarf as a sling.

"Please come in, girls," she said warmly, brushing a wisp of grey hair out of her eyes. "You'll have to pardon my appearance—and the appearance of this house, too—but it's hard to keep things in order when you only have one hand and arm to do it with."

She laughed nervously, and ushered Trixie and Honey into a cozy, cluttered living room. All the surfaces were piled high with magazines and books.

Suddenly, a small black-and-white dog came tearing around the corner, yapping furiously. His stiff brush of wiry fur seemed to be standing on end with anger as he planted his feet firmly in front of Trixie and Honey.

"Oh, Willy," Mrs. De Keyser said. "Stop all that noise! These nice girls have come to help me, you silly thing."

Willy cocked his head to one side, but was not about to change his mind.

"Oh, he won't bite," Mrs. De Keyser said, patting his head fondly. "He just likes to make a fuss when someone new comes into the house. Poor thing—he gets so bored, especially now that I can't take him for such long walks."

"We'll take him for you," said Trixie, smiling and bending down to pat the dog on the head. Willy growled slightly, and then rolled over on his back. He grinned a dog grin at her and begged to have his tummy scratched.

"There, you see?" Mrs. De Keyser said. "He likes you. I knew he would. He really likes young people a great deal."

"Do you want to tell us what chores need to be done?" asked Honey politely, putting down her books and slipping out of her jacket. "We should get started, especially if there are a lot."

"Oh, yes, of course," Mrs. De Keyser said. "Here, hang your coats up in this closet— that is, if you can find a hanger. Oh dear, what a mess. I was planning to straighten out the closets, and then this dreadful thing happened."

She waved her cast mournfully at them, but perked right up again.

"Actually, the first thing you can do is follow me around the house, and move the things that I use a lot into my reach." She went into the kitchen, and the two girls trailed behind her. "You see, I have difficulty getting at the things I need every day."

"Do you want anyone to help you with yard work?" Trixie asked. "I have two older brothers, and they'll be glad to come and rake the leaves or trim the hedges for you."

"Well, isn't that sweet of them," the older woman said gratefully. "But the outdoor work can wait. What I really need you for is to help me tidy up, put things away, and make the bed. Perhaps you can also help me prepare a big stew so I can just heat a little up now and then when I get hungry."

"We'd love to!" Trixie said briskly. "Where should we start?"

"I think we should prepare the stew," said Honey. "Then we can dust and vacuum while it's cooking."

"Aren't you wonderful," Mrs. De Keyser said. "Now, I have everything right here in the fridge! Mrs. Vanderpoel did a big shopping for me, and we had it delivered. That's all very nice, but how can I be expected to slice onions and carrots with one hand, I ask you?"

Mrs. De Keyser opened the refrigerator door and bent down to get some vegetables. A bag of carrots dropped on the floor. In a flash, Willy zipped over and grabbed the bag.

"Now, Willy! You come back here with those carrots this instant!" Mrs. De Keyser snapped, straightening up. "That dog just loves to snatch things. I'm always finding the strangest things in the most unexpected places. Willy! Bring that here this minute!"

But Willy, loving the game, dashed back into the living room with Trixie on his heels. He ran around behind the couch. Seconds later, he emerged with dust bunnies on the end of his nose, and a look of triumph on his face.

Trixie, not fooled for a minute, reached her arm behind the couch and pulled out the bag of carrots.

"Naughty dog!" she scolded sternly. But Willy just wagged his tail and dashed back into the kitchen.

Following Mrs. De Keyser's careful instructions, the girls put the meat and vegetables they'd sliced into a heavy Dutch oven along with some spices. Then they followed her up to the second floor of the house and got out the vacuum cleaner. Trixie quickly began to vacuum Mrs. De Keyser's bedroom, while Honey straightened the bedclothes and plumped the pillows.

"Now you're sure this isn't too much for you?" Mrs. De Keyser asked.

"It's not hard," Trixie said, smiling. "We thought we'd come every day after school and do things for you."

"Oh, my goodness," she answered. "That really isn't necessary. I'll manage quite nicely on all you've done here today."

"Oh, no," Honey said. "I think we should come at least every other day, don't you, Trixie?"

Trixie bent her head in concentration as she stuck the vacuum cleaner nozzle behind a chair cushion.

"We can come as often as you need us, Mrs. De Keyser," she said. "Every other day would be fine with us."

"Are you sure?" Mrs. De Keyser asked. "I certainly wouldn't want to trouble you."

"It's no trouble, Mrs. De Keyser," said Trixie, turning off the vacuum cleaner. "Besides, we are grateful for the chance to get off the bus here. We've been meaning to stop and have a look at the new antique store."

"Oh yes . . ." Mrs. De Keyser began, then her voice trailed off. A frown creased her brow at the mention of the antique shop.

"Have you been inside yet?" Trixie asked.

She wondered why Mrs. De Keyser seemed so troubled.

"Yes, only briefly. Oh, I do so worry about that man," Mrs. De Keyser said in a sad voice. "You know, I rented that barn to Mr. Reid, and I thought it would make a lovely shop. But now I'm not so sure. It's right on Glen Road, but so far he's had hardly any customers at all. I wonder how he affords the rent."

"He doesn't look as if he's doing so badly," Trixie muttered, thinking about the expensive car he drove.

"Well, I mentioned it to the real estate agent, but she said I was being silly to even consider reducing the rent. I suppose it is silly of me because he always pays on time."

"Well, maybe things will be better in the summer when more tourists are on the road," Honey said reassuringly.

"Yes, that's what I keep telling myself," Mrs. De Keyser said. "After all, he has a whole store full of antiques to sell. But, you know, he's hardly ever open and I never see any customers!"

"Do you like antiques?" Trixie asked. "We certainly do."

Mrs. De Keyser stopped, and then burst into a merry laugh.

"Oh, my dear. Like antiques?" Her small round form shook with laughter. "Not really. You see, when you get to be my age, an antique is just something that was brand-new when you were young. Some things, of course, are much older than that, but those generally aren't the ones that turn up in antique stores."

Trixie and Honey smiled at Mrs. De Keyser. Then Willy suddenly jumped up, scratching at their skirts.

"Oh dear," Mrs. De Keyser gasped, catching her breath. "I forgot all about poor Willy. I know it's getting to be five o'clock, but would you be dears and take him for a little walk outside? And don't let him off the leash. The silly thing likes to run off and explore. Sometimes he doesn't come back for hours at a time."

Trixie and Honey got their jackets from the closet, and put Willy on his leash. They stepped outside and breathed in the crisp air. It was early November and most of the leaves had fallen from the trees. The branches looked like spidery drawings

against the sky. They shuffled through the
dry leaves as they walked. Their red and
gold colors had long ago turned to brown,
and they blanketed the lawn and the bushes
around the house.

Trixie and Honey welcomed the chance to
be outside and to look all around Mrs. De
Keyser's snug little house. To the north
stood a long row of fir trees. They had probably been planted a hundred years ago to
break the cold north wind that blew all winter. Rhododendrons and azalea bushes snuggled up against the graceful porch, and a
broad, curly maple tree grew on the front
lawn.

"Willy probably wishes he could find a
nice rabbit to play with," Honey said, as the
surprisingly strong dog dragged her from one
bush to the next, looking for good things to
sniff.

Willy led the girls to the south side of the
property, and they found themselves standing about two hundred yards from The Antique Barn. Trixie and Honey stood there
quietly, gazing wistfully at the warm yellow
light that spilled from the windows. They
could see someone moving inside.

"Look, Honey. It's open. Why don't we stop in?" said Trixie, excitement mounting in her voice. "After we leave Mrs. De Keyser's, we can have a quick look before we head home."

3 * The Curious
Antique Shop

TRIXIE AND HONEY took Willy back inside,
then made sure that everything Mrs. De
Keyser would need the next day was within
easy reach. They put the stew in several
smaller containers in the refrigerator, and
washed the heavy Dutch oven.

"You girls have really done a wonderful
job," Mrs. De Keyser said as she gazed
around her somewhat tidier house. "I don't
know how to thank you enough."

"Actually," Trixie said, picking up her

books, "you've taught us how to make a terrific stew."

"I'm going right home and write down the recipe," Honey added. "I don't think I ever smelled anything quite that good."

"Maybe our payment should be special cooking lessons," Trixie suggested. "Not that we need any payment, of course."

"Dr. Ferris said you were sweet girls," Mrs. De Keyser said as she walked them to the door. "But he didn't say *how* sweet."

Willy started to bark as the girls stepped out onto the porch and said good-night.

"He doesn't want you to leave," Mrs. De Keyser said. She bent down and patted Willy on the head. "Now don't worry, the girls will be back day after tomorrow."

Willy kept barking furiously as the door closed, and Trixie skipped down the steps ahead of her friend.

"Now, let's take a quick look in The Antique Barn," she whispered. "Oh, I hope it's still open."

Honey and Trixie quickly crossed the lawn, and then walked along the few feet of road that separated them from the interesting little shop. They climbed the wooden steps in front, and gasped as they looked in the window.

Behind the small leaded panes of the big bay window was a display of antique dolls and toys. Worn-out teddy bears leaned up against glamorous china-headed dolls and wooden trains. A good-sized dollhouse was set in the corner, and tiny little beaded lamps illuminated its little rooms. Further into the shop, they could see delicate pieces of furniture, oriental rugs, a lace-covered canopy bed, and iron pots and pans. Trixie felt a smile begin to crease her lips at the sight.

Unable to resist, Trixie opened the door and the girls stepped into the cluttered shop. As the door shut behind them, a loud bell clanged in the back of the store.

They stood uncertainly in the center of the large room for a moment, but no one appeared. They turned toward the window display to have a better look at the enchanting toys.

Trixie put down her books and picked up an odd-looking contraption.

"Look at this, Honey," she whispered. "What do you think it could be?"

Standing on a cast-iron base was a little iron man with his hand outstretched. A small cast-iron barrel stood on the base about two inches away from him.

Honey was something of an expert on antiques. "I think it's a bank," she answered, after taking a closer look. "I saw one at the museum once. You're supposed to put a penny on the man's hand. Then you pull this lever, and he throws the coin into the barrel."

Amazed, Trixie replaced the bank, and looked around her.

"Honey," she said. "I think that one must be a bank, too!"

On a shelf against the wall, between a wooden train set and a toy ship, stood another mechanical toy. On its small rectangular platform, an Indian knelt, facing a bear. The Indian held a gun.

"I bet the Indian shoots the penny into the bear!"

Honey laughed, and then turned to look at a small toy mule pulling a two-wheeled cart. She was about to wind the toy up just to see what it did, when suddenly they heard a noise behind them.

"Can I help you?" came a low, gravelly voice.

Both girls turned around to face the owner of the voice.

"Uh, yes," Trixie stammered.

A short, stocky, middle-aged man faced the girls. He was wearing an expensive-looking, perfectly fitted grey suit. A gleaming gold chain rested across his slight paunch.

"We were just looking at the toys," Trixie explained. "They're very interesting. We were wondering if the Indian and the bear were a bank of some sort."

"A bank?" the man said. "I have no idea."

"What is this donkey supposed to do?" Honey asked, holding up the small toy. "Would it be all right if I wound it up?"

"No, I'd rather you didn't," the man muttered. "It's an antique, and it might break."

"Of course," Honey said, putting the toy down. "Then could you tell me where this dollhouse comes from? It looks as if it might have been made in the 1880's, but the way the roof is made makes me think it might have been later."

The man frowned and rubbed his cheek thoughtfully. He looked from the dollhouse to Honey, as if undecided about what to say.

Honey pretended not to notice his discomfort, and went right on asking questions. She moved quickly around the room, touching one object after another, while Trixie watched the man's reactions in amazement. Honey was miles ahead of him in her knowledge of antiques.

While the man was distracted, Trixie studied his face. Could he be the owner? She really hadn't been able to see the face of the man driving the maroon Mercedes-Benz, so perhaps this wasn't Mr. Reid at all.

"Is Mr. Reid here?" she asked finally.

"I'm Carl Reid," he answered. "What do you want?"

"You're the owner?" Trixie gasped. "I mean, uh, are you in charge of running this store?"

"Yes, I am," Carl Reid answered gruffly.

Honey, embarrassed by Trixie's blunder, stepped forward to take over the conversation. She thought it was certainly odd that Mr. Reid didn't know anything about his merchandise, but maybe there was a good reason. He may have taken over someone else's profitable business, as an investment. Her father did that sometimes.

"We wanted to know about the china dolls," Honey said smoothly. "I have a friend who's a collector, but she's looking for dolls made in Germany before 1885."

"Really, kid," Mr. Reid said, and he rolled his eyes up to the ceiling in annoyance. "I can't help you. Your friend would just have to come in here and see for herself."

"When was this battleship made?" Honey asked. She couldn't resist another question. "Is it supposed to be a Civil War ship?"

Mr. Reid looked blank and then his eyes narrowed slightly. He glanced nervously behind him into the storage room.

"Why don't you be nice kids and go home?" he said, smiling sweetly all of a sudden. "I'm busy in the back right now, and I really can't take the time to chat."

"But I wanted to ask you about the—" Trixie broke off when she felt Honey's hand on her arm.

"Thank you very much for your time," Honey said, and she led Trixie to the door. "It was very nice of you to let us look around."

"Sure thing," Mr. Reid said. He seemed relieved. "Anytime."

"Honey!" Trixie snapped, as the door

closed after them. "Why did you drag me out of there? I wanted to keep looking at the antiques!"

"I'm sorry, Trixie," Honey said, "but it was obvious that Mr. Reid didn't want us in there anymore. Besides, it's getting dark and we should be starting home."

Trixie kicked at the stones along the side of the road as they walked. She knew that Honey was right, but she was very curious about Mr. Reid, too.

"Didn't you find it a bit peculiar that he didn't know anything about antiques?" Trixie asked finally.

"Well, for one thing," Honey said, "you can't jump to conclusions about his knowledge of antiques. Just because he didn't know about the toys, doesn't mean he knows nothing about any antiques at all."

"Yes, I know," Trixie said, "but I think you and I know more about antiques than Mr. Reid does. You do anyway."

"You're still jumping to conclusions, Trixie. He's a businessman. He knew we weren't planning to buy anything from the shop. He didn't want us wasting his time unless we were serious!"

"Humph," Trixie sniffed, feeling somewhat put out. "I'm always serious! I just think there's something fishy about that man, that's all."

"That's what I love about you, Trixie Belden," Honey said. She threw an arm around Trixie's shoulders and gave her a brief hug. "If it wasn't for you, our lives would be so dull and boring!"

"I don't think up things that are fishy, Honey Wheeler," Trixie said, defending herself. "I only notice them!"

"Well, I'm beginning to notice a strange cold feeling in the area of my feet," Honey said. "I'm going to run the rest of the way home. Beat you!"

And with that, Honey started to run as fast as she could along Glen Road. It was a long way, however, and she soon slowed to a walk. Trixie caught up to her, and together they walked until they came to the driveway of the Manor House where Honey lived.

They were panting with exertion from the brisk walk, but feeling a good deal warmer.

"Why don't you come to our house for dinner?" Trixie asked.

"Great idea," Honey replied. "I'll call

Miss Trask from your house."

Miss Trask was Honey's governess, and she also managed the Wheeler estate. Honey adored Miss Trask, as did all the Bob-Whites.

"Good thinking," Trixie said. "Race you to the front door!"

The two girls set off again. They clambered up the steps of Trixie's house, and fell against the door in unison, laughing.

Moments later, the door was opened by Brian Belden, but he wasn't quick enough to protect the girls from their greatest admirer—Reddy!

"Down boy!" Trixie shouted, but it was too late. Reddy, the Belden's handsome Irish setter, leapt on them, and showered the girls with dog kisses. Trixie's books fell to the floor, and the papers in her loose-leaf notebook went flying for the third time in two days.

"Is that you, Trixie?" Mrs. Belden called from the kitchen.

"Yes Moms. Sorry we're a little late," Trixie called back, bending down to pick up her books. Reddy trampled through the papers excitedly.

Trixie went into the kitchen. "Hi, Moms, Hi, Dad," she said, giving each a kiss. "May Honey stay for dinner?"

"Of course, but wash up first," Mrs. Belden answered. "Dinner will be on the table in three minutes. Call Miss Trask, Honey. She's waiting to hear from you."

Honey quickly sidestepped the mess Reddy had made of Trixie's papers, and went to phone Miss Trask for permission to stay for dinner. By the time she'd completed the phone call and washed her hands, the family was seated at the table.

"And then Willy, the dog, stole the carrots," Trixie was saying, as she picked up her fork.

"Pass the mashed potatoes, please," Mart mumbled, as he set down the platter of fried chicken.

"And Mrs. De Keyser taught us how to make the greatest stew," Trixie continued. "She's teaching us how to cook. We're going to prepare meals for her in advance, so she can heat things up when she gets hungry."

"Well, isn't that nice, dear," Mrs. Belden said. "And did you get a chance to look at the antique store?"

"I was just getting to that, Moms," Trixie said. "We paid Mr. Carl Reid of The Antique Barn a visit all right, but he doesn't know *a thing* about antiques! Can you believe it? We asked him quite a few questions about the dolls and toys in his window display, and he couldn't answer one of them!"

"Oh no," Brian groaned. "Here we go again!"

"Is our inquisitive sibling trying to initiate another second-rate series of innuendos?" Mart muttered. But he smiled affectionately at his suspicious sister. "Who knows what evil lurks in the hearts of antique dealers—or where it will lead."

"Mart!" Trixie said, feeling insulted. "My innuendos are *never* second-rate! How dare you!"

"Crooks, beware!" Mart intoned in a somber voice. "The schoolgirl shamus is on the trail again!"

"Trixie thinks it's highly irregular and cause for suspicion if a person who knows nothing about antiques is in the antique business, that's all," Brian said.

"Well, I know how you feel, Trixie," Mr. Belden said. He had been listening with interest. "But nowadays, there are a lot of people in business who know nothing about what they're trying to make or sell. Many people believe that any business can be reduced to numbers, and columns of figures. It's what is called 'the bottom line.'"

"You mean, Daddy, that lots of people go into businesses just for the money?" Trixie asked.

"That's right, sweetie," Mr. Belden said. He paused briefly. "So, even though *you* think it's suspicious for Mr. Reid not to know about antiques, at the bank we see that as an everyday occurrence."

"But Mrs. De Keyser says he doesn't even have customers!" Trixie said. "What kind of a business is that? I still think it's strange, and I'm going to investigate some more."

Her eyes flashed as she looked around the table. "Believe me, you'll see who's right!"

4 * Trixie Investigates

THE FOLLOWING DAY after school, Trixie and Honey decided they'd better devote their entire afternoon to studying the list of spelling words for the contest. Mart insisted on helping them—in between his huge snacks—but Trixie complained that he was not being entirely helpful.

"You're just showing off, Mart," Honey agreed, laughing. "We all know that you know a lot of big words, but I'll bet you that the word *prestidigitator* isn't anywhere on that list!"

"It is inconsequential and irrelevant to worry about things like that!" said Mart. "How you can even begin to lay claim to the exalted position of local spelling finalist and potential Eastern Regional winner, without a thorough knowledge of spelling, is beyond me."

"You just want us to know you can pronounce that word!" Trixie argued.

"Oh, by the way, ladies," Mart said, faking a tremendous yawn, "I forgot to mention your newspaper assignments."

Trixie picked up one of the couch pillows and tossed it at Mart's head.

"Forgot?" she howled, as she took aim with another pillow. "How could you *forget* something like that? I have half a mind to bury you in feathers!"

"Now don't get excited! The articles aren't due for three weeks, so try and be temperate. Smooth your ruffled feathers!"

Honey, acting like an island of sanity in a sea of hysteria, grabbed the pillow from Trixie's hand and sat on it.

"Just tell us the assignment," she said merrily. "Unless you've forgotten what it is."

"I most certainly didn't forget what it is,"

Mart said pompously. "We're each supposed to choose a local merchant, and interview them about what they sell and how seasonal buying habits affect their merchandise. And at the same time we're supposed to encourage them to take out ads in the school paper."

"Oh boy, that's a hard one," Trixie muttered. "They want interviews? What if the storekeepers don't have time to talk to us?"

"What if we don't have time to talk to the storekeepers?" Honey asked.

"Well, a newspaper can't consist entirely of editorials, can it? Just because an opinion is easier to get down on paper doesn't mean that's what the people want to read about, little sister. Hieroglyphics."

"I beg your pardon?"

"Hieroglyphics. It's the next word on the list, so start spelling!"

"H-e-i-r-o-g-l-i—"

"You might as well stop right there, because you're way off," Mart said. "You've already made two errors, and you're not even finished with the word yet."

"Let me try," Honey said, frowning slightly and closing her eyes to concentrate. "H-i-e-r-o-g-l-i—"

"You're both hopeless," Mart said, throwing down the pillow he'd been holding. "I really doubt that either of you will win this contest. As a matter of fact, it completely escapes me how you even got to be local finalists."

Trixie started to throw the pillow she was holding at him, when suddenly she stopped. A bubble of laughter caught in her throat, and then Honey and Trixie began to giggle uncontrollably.

"You're just jealous, Mart," Honey teased. "Don't worry. If one of us wins, we'll let you keep the trophy in your room, okay?"

"Perhaps you should win it first—then we'll discuss who gets to keep it!" Mart said. "I'm going out to practice basketball. You two don't appreciate my attempts at your edification, that much is clear."

"That's not true," Trixie had to admit. "We're glad you want to help us. By the way, that word is spelled e-d-i-f-i-c-a-t-i-o-n, for your edification!"

Mart laughed. "See you later," he called, and went to get his jacket.

The girls settled down to some serious studying. They covered every word on the list twice—once for Honey, and once for

Trixie. All the while, they could hear the wop-wop sound the basketball made on the driveway.

"Studying together is so much fun," Honey said, "but I think I'd better head home now, Trixie. Miss Trask already thinks I've moved in with the Belden family! Besides, I promised I'd set up a schedule with Regan for exercising the horses."

"Did you tell him that we promised to help Mrs. De Keyser every other day?" Trixie asked, pained at having neglected one of her other chores—and a favorite one, at that. All the Bob-Whites helped exercise the horses in the Wheeler stables. Honey, who was an excellent equestrienne, had taught Trixie how to ride. Trixie loved riding, and felt very bad about neglecting the horses.

"Is Regan angry at us?" she asked.

"No," Honey said, as she slipped on her jacket. "Regan's very pleased that we're helping someone, but the horses need to get exercised, too. Jim and Dan are helping, but you and I should also do our share."

"No problem," Trixie said, walking Honey to the door. "I'll do whatever I can. See you tomorrow morning on the bus!"

She waved, and then watched Honey cut across the back of the property and take the foot path to the Manor House.

Later that night, after Trixie had eaten, done the rest of her homework, and helped her mother with the dinner dishes, she went upstairs with Bobby and read him a story before bed. She watched his eyelids grow heavier and heavier. When it looked as if he could hold out against sleep no longer, she turned off the lamp and kissed him goodnight.

In her room, Trixie lay waiting for sleep, but her mind was so full of dancing thoughts that she only felt more awake than ever. There was so much to do: Mrs. De Keyser, the horses, the Eastern Regional—and she had all her usual chores, and homework too!

And the newspaper assignment. She'd almost forgotten that.

Suddenly her eyes flew open. *I've got it!* she thought. *I'm surprised I didn't think of it before! I'll interview Carl Reid for the school newspaper. It's a perfect excuse for snooping around and it will make a really good article, too. I'll bet I'm not the only one who's interested in those old-time toys.*

Trixie settled back against the pillow, and reviewed the wonderful banks and mechanical toys she'd only had a brief chance to look at. *Each one is practically an invention in itself!* she thought happily. *Why, I'd interview Mr. Reid even if he wasn't suspicious, but this only makes it better.*

Trixie snuggled under the covers, and fell asleep contemplating her plan.

The next day after school, Trixie and Honey got off the bus at Mrs. De Keyser's house, and spent an hour helping her. They did some laundry and took care of the pile of dishes that had accumulated in the last two days.

"Oh dear," Mrs. De Keyser fussed. "I'm so embarrassed about this mess, but if I do dishes, I just know I'll get my cast all wet. What a nuisance!"

"Please, don't give it a thought, Mrs. De Keyser," Honey said soothingly. "If you could do these things yourself, then there'd be no need for us to come and help. We really do understand."

"Oh, I know you do, dear." The distraught woman smiled at the girls. "Now, when my arm is better I'm going to invite you over for tea some afternoon. Then I'll have a chance to do something for you!"

"We'd love it," Trixie said. "And besides, we're going to miss Willy, so we were hoping you'd invite us over to play with him sometimes."

Willy, who had been running circles around Trixie as she dusted, started yapping enthusiastically.

"Poor Willy will miss you, too," Mrs. De Keyser said gratefully. "Now, I really feel bad about keeping you two busy girls here any longer. Why don't you run along, and I'll see you again day after tomorrow."

Trixie and Honey collected their books and put on their coats. After the door closed behind them, Trixie explained her plan about the interview to Honey.

Honey hesitated. "I don't know, Trixie," she said. "Mr. Reid wasn't too eager to talk the last time."

"But this is different," Trixie insisted. "If I do an article about the shop, it will probably attract customers. Then Mr. Reid will make more money. Why, I'll bet a lot of people don't even know the store is here. Glen Road isn't exactly a main thoroughfare, you know."

"Perhaps you're right," Honey said, understanding her friend's persistence. "Why don't you go ahead and do the interview now? I have to go home and help Miss Trask with the mending."

"Okay, Honey," Trixie said. "Who are you planning to interview?"

"I was thinking of interviewing the butcher," Honey said, trying to suppress a giggle. "He's going to say, 'I buy lots of turkeys at Thanksgiving and lots of hams at Christmas, and thank you very much but I most definitely *don't* want to take out an ad in the Sleepyside Junior-Senior High School newspaper!'"

Trixie waved to her friend as Honey skipped up the road. Then she turned her attention to the task at hand—Mr. Carl Reid and his antique store!

Her heart beat fast as she went next door to the shop. But her excitement quickly turned to dismay when she saw the "Closed" sign hanging in the window. *It's not even late*, she thought grumpily. *How on earth does Mr. Reid ever expect to make any money if he doesn't keep his shop open?*

Pressing her face against the glass-paned door, she tried desperately to see inside the darkened shop. There was a tiny light on in the back. She pulled at the bell rope and banged on the door, but no one answered.

I just know someone's back there! Trixie thought. *But whoever it is just isn't in the mood to answer the doorbell.* She knocked loudly a few more times, and then sat down on the step disconsolately. But she was deterred for only a minute. *Why not just go around to the back and check to see if anyone's there?* she asked herself. *After all, my name wouldn't be Trixie Belden if I just sat on the steps and did nothing.*

Trixie picked up her books, and marched around to the back of the shop. Small windows were set rather low in the side and back of the wooden building, and the rear door was the old-fashioned Dutch kind. The top could swing open separately from the bottom, but today they were both shut, and locked.

Trixie pressed her face against one of the small windows and tried to make out the objects in the dimly lit room. A bare overhead bulb gave off enough light for her to distinguish some of the shapes. She could see a small Queen Anne sofa, with springs popping through the horsehair. There was also a pile of old leather-bound books atop a handsome bureau with brass drawer pulls. Farther in the corner, she could see an old record player—the kind with a horn—sitting on what appeared to be an antique printing press.

Trixie knocked on the window, but it was obvious the store was empty. *Too bad!* Trixie thought sadly. *This would have been a perfect opportunity to do the interview—if only someone were here to answer the questions!*

Deciding to give up and go home, she turned and found herself face to face with Mr. Reid.

"What do you mean snooping around here!" he shouted.

"I was just . . ." Trixie stammered, trying to collect her thoughts.

But evidently, Mr. Reid wasn't through with his tirade.

"You have some nerve, kid," he yelled. "You know, trespassing is against the law around here!"

Trixie stood rooted to the spot.

"But I wasn't—I mean, I wanted to talk to you. I was just looking . . ."

Her voice trailed off as she saw the unreasoning anger on Mr. Reid's face.

"Listen, kid, don't poke your nose into other people's business, you got that?"

"Yes, sir, but—"

"But nothing. Now please leave!"

Trixie didn't waste any more time trying to explain. She turned and ran down Glen Road as fast as she could. She didn't stop running until she reached the driveway of Crabapple Farm.

She was frightened, but angry too. *After all*, she thought, as she tried to catch her breath, *what's a person supposed to do in an antique shop? Snoop and browse, that's what! What a horrible man!*

Trixie stomped into the house and dropped her books on the hall table. Without even taking off her coat, she rushed over to the telephone and called Honey. She could hardly wait to hear the excuses Honey would come up with this time for Mr. Reid's impossible behavior.

5 * An Unusual Favor

TRIXIE TRIED to tell Honey about Mr. Reid, but never got a word in edgewise. The minute Honey heard her voice on the telephone, she started talking.

"Oh Trixie, I was about to call you! You'll never guess what!" Honey's voice was a high-pitched rush of excitement. "Daddy and Mommy have just given me the most wonderful news!"

"Quick, tell me!" Trixie gasped, instantly forgetting why she'd called Honey in the first place.

"Well," Honey went on breathlessly, "you know how this is a long weekend because of the teacher conferences? Well, Daddy has to go to Paris, and guess what? They said they're so proud of me for being a finalist in the spelling contest, and getting sent to the Eastern Regional—oh, this is so exciting I can barely talk."

"Come on, Honey," Trixie begged. "Now you've got me all excited too!"

"Wait till you hear! You'll never guess. They want me to go with them, and you too!"

"I don't believe it!" Trixie yelped. "Whoopee! Are you sure they really want me to come too?"

"Of course, silly," Honey said. "After all, you're the person who made it all possible. I mean, you're the one who helped me get over my shyness and everything!"

"Oh, Honey," Trixie murmured. "I don't know what to say!"

"Of course you know what to say!" Honey giggled. "You're supposed to say yes!"

"Yes! I mean, I guess so. I have to ask Moms, though."

"Well, then, go ask her!" said Honey. "Oh,

I'm so excited. Hurry!"

Trixie let the phone receiver drop to the floor with a clunk as she raced into the kitchen to speak to her mother.

Helen Belden listened quietly to the rush of words that spilled out of her excited daughter.

"Well, dear, I don't know what to say," she began. "It's rather embarrassing, you know, such a large gift. There would be no way on earth we could ever do something similar for Honey."

"Mo-o-ms!" Trixie groaned. "Please, pretty please with honey and sugar and tons of extra chores on top. *Please?*"

Mrs. Belden smiled as she watched her daughter writhe with anxiety. "I guess so, dear. You tell Honey I said it was fine, but I would like to speak with her mother this evening. Is that all right?"

Trixie raced back to the telephone and gave Honey the good news.

"We can still study this weekend, too. After all, we'll be together, won't we?" Trixie reminded her friend.

"That's right," Honey answered. "What else is there to do in Paris besides study for a spelling test?"

Trixie's peal of laughter could be heard all the way to Glen Road, but suddenly she stopped.

"Oh, my goodness," she gasped. "I forgot all about Mrs. De Keyser!"

"I didn't," Honey said calmly. "Jim isn't coming with us because of the big basketball game this weekend. He promised me that he and Mart and Brian will go over Sunday morning and help Mrs. De Keyser."

"Will they be able to cook for her?" Trixie asked, wondering if Mrs. De Keyser would have enough food to hold her over the long weekend.

"Why not?" Honey answered. "Jim is actually a pretty good cook. There's no reason why Brian and Mart can't learn something useful, too."

"You're absolutely right, Honey. I think this will be a broadening experience for them!"

"Now here's my plan," began Honey, getting more serious. "We'll stop at Mrs. De Keyser's house after school tomorrow and do a few quick things. Then you go home and pack. Friday night, you'll come here for dinner. Afterwards Tom will take us in the limousine to Westchester Airport. We're taking off at about 11 o'clock, and we'll be in Paris by morning."

"We're flying at night?" Trixie marveled. "When will we sleep?"

"We'll sleep on the plane, silly," Honey said with a laugh. "It takes six hours to fly across the Atlantic, but Europe is six hours ahead of the United States. We'll arrive in Paris at 5 o'clock in the morning, New York time. But it will be 11 o'clock in the morning, Paris time."

"That's too confusing for me, Honey," Trixie said. "I only hope the seats in the plane are comfortable."

"Don't worry," Honey said. "They lean way back and turn into beds. We'll sleep like babies."

Visions of the Eiffel Tower and famous painters in Left Bank cafes whirled through Trixie's head that night. When she finally fell asleep, her dreams were filled with exotic-looking tourists and a hundred varieties of French pastries. She woke up feeling as if she'd already been to Paris and back—all in one night.

The next day at school passed in a blur, as Trixie moved from class to class like a wooden statue. More than once, she was scolded by her teachers for not paying attention.

After school, she and Honey did some quick housework for Mrs. De Keyser, but their minds weren't on their jobs. Mrs. De Keyser noticed, and was infected by their excitement.

"Oh, how wonderful it is to be young," Mrs. De Keyser said. "I remember the first time I went to Paris, as if it were yesterday. You girls are going to have a splendid time."

Trixie whirled around the living room with the vacuum cleaner as if it were a dancing partner. Willy, overexcited by all the giggling and silliness, jumped up onto the coffee table and grabbed the feather duster. Snarling happily at it, he dashed around the corner and went racing up the stairs.

"Willy!" Honey shouted. "I saw that, you sneaky little dog! Come back here!"

She dashed upstairs after him, and retrieved the duster before he could do any damage.

"I believe he thought it was a chicken," Honey joked. "I think we should take him out for a run to make up for the loss of the feather duster!"

Trixie and Honey put on their jackets and

ran all over the backyard with Willy. Hoping
to exhaust him, they took turns running him
from one side of the hedge to the other. But
they only succeeded in exhausting themselves. Laughing and gasping for breath,
they sank down on the lawn to rest. Trixie
stuck her foot through the loop in Willy's
leash to prevent him from running off.

"Now tell me again," she panted. "What
are we going to do when we get to France?"

"Well, for one thing," Honey said, "we'll
still be on New York time and we might be
really tired. But we probably will want to go
sight-seeing anyway. So first we'll go on that
glass-covered boat on the Seine, and then
we'll go to the top of the Eiffel Tower, and
then we'll eat in a nice sidewalk cafe, and
then we'll go to this wonderful museum
called the Louvre, and then—"

"Stop!" Trixie said, falling over backwards
in mock exhaustion. She flung her arms out
on either side of her into a heap of dry
leaves. "I can't stand it. It's too much. Paris!
How lucky can I get?"

"Did I hear you say Paris?" came a familiar gravelly voice from the hedge next to
them. Willy started barking, but Honey

stroked the little dog's head, until he finally calmed down.

"Why, hello, Mr. Reid," Honey said sweetly. "Yes, we were talking about Paris."

"I couldn't help overhearing your conversation," he said in an unusually friendly tone. He smiled warmly, and leaned forward a bit. "You wouldn't happen to be going there soon, would you?"

"As a matter of fact," Trixie said haughtily, "we're leaving tomorrow evening."

Remembering how nasty he had been to her the day before, Trixie wondered why Mr. Reid was so interested in their talk about Paris, and why he was being so nice all of a sudden. The other day he had thought she was nothing but a pesky teen-ager. Now, Trixie didn't feel inclined to be polite. She wanted Mr. Reid to know she was a person to be reckoned with!

"We happen to be flying to Paris in Mr. Wheeler's *private* jet, Mr. Reid," she continued, her nose held at a lofty angle.

"How exciting for you girls," Mr. Reid said in his most charming voice. "Have you been to Paris before?"

Both Trixie and Honey answered at the

same time. "Yes," said Honey. "No," said
Trixie. And before they knew it, they were
having a very chatty conversation about vari-
ous galleries and restaurants that Mr. Reid
felt they should visit.

"Please call me Carl," he said finally, after
learning their names. "And now that I see
what nice young ladies you are, I wonder if I
might ask a favor of you?"

Trixie tilted her head to one side, suddenly curious. She wondered what kind of
favor he had in mind. Honey seemed to have
no reservations, but she hadn't been yelled
at, either. In all the excitement, Trixie hadn't
gotten around to telling her the whole story
of her disastrous encounter with Mr. Reid.

"Of course," Honey said. "If we can, we'd
be happy to do a favor for you."

"Well, I know it might be a lot to ask," Mr.
Reid went on, "but you could be a great help
to me. You see, a friend of mine has found
the most exquisite antique doll. It's now in
Paris and I was planning to ship it air ex-
press. Unfortunately, so many things get broken when you ship them. They have no re-
spect for other people's property in those
baggage areas."

Trixie nodded as she listened to Mr. Reid. She had heard other adults say that about freight depots.

"I was just wondering," he continued, "if it would be possible for you to bring the doll back to the United States for me? I would feel so much better knowing that it was in safe hands in a private plane, instead of being bounced around in the hold of one of those jumbo jets. She's absolutely irreplaceable, and if she should be broken, well . . ."

"We'd be delighted to, Mr. Reid—I mean, Carl," Honey said politely.

"I'll go inside and write down the address. I'll also give you a note to deliver when you get there," Mr. Reid said blandly. "I feel I can trust you to handle this."

"I'm glad we can help you," Trixie said, somewhat flattered at his praise. Trixie watched as Mr. Reid went into the shop. She'd almost, but not quite, forgotten how grouchy he had been. She still thought it was odd that he hadn't known the answers to any of their questions about the antique toys, but perhaps Honey was right. Maybe he didn't know that much about the antique toys, although he certainly seemed awfully interested in this particular doll.

Sometimes it was so hard to tell with grown-ups, she thought, heaving a great sigh. *One minute they were grouchy, and the next minute they were as sweet as sugar.*

She turned to Honey as soon as Mr. Reid was inside the shop. "Do you really think it'll be all right if we pick up this doll for him?" she whispered.

"I don't see why not," Honey answered. "After all, it won't take too much time to just stop off somewhere. Besides, we might get to see a really interesting French antique store."

"That's true," Trixie mused. "I hadn't thought of that."

Carl Reid returned and handed a piece of paper and a sealed envelope to Honey.

"This one is the address, and this is a short note," he said. "Now just give the envelope to André when you see him, and he will give you the doll."

He cut his smile short, and turned as if to leave. But just as quickly he turned back. "It would be better if you didn't take the doll out of the case," he said. There was a weak smile on his lips and Trixie couldn't explain the cold feeling she got in the pit of her stomach. "You see, she's packed very carefully. If she isn't put back in correctly, she'll shake loose and break."

"We understand," Honey said, trying to sound reassuring. "We'll just bring her straight to you."

"Thank you," Mr. Reid said, and with another brief look in their direction, he went into the shop.

"He's an odd bird," Trixie said, after she and Honey had taken Willy back inside, and said good-bye to Mrs. De Keyser. They walked quickly along Glen Road.

"Yes, he is a bit odd," agreed Honey. "But lots of times people act strangely. Maybe he's unhappy about something. Who knows?"

"And, actually, who cares," Trixie said. "I'll worry about his problems after this weekend. Right now, I have too many exciting things on my mind."

The two girls walked home together, and then said good-night. Trixie spent the evening choosing and then discarding clothes to take on the trip. Soon she had a suitcase stuffed with clothes, but her room looked as

if a cyclone had struck. Promising herself
that she'd get up early the next morning and
tidy up, Trixie fell into an exhausted sleep.

The next day at school went by so slowly,
Trixie was convinced that someone had
poured molasses into all the clocks. But, finally, the school bus dropped Honey, Trixie,
Mart, and Brian off at their stop. The boys
immediately headed up the driveway, leaving Honey and Trixie at the mailbox.

"Friday night is finally here," Trixie said
happily. "I thought I'd never get through the
day!"

"Me, too!" Honey said. "Let's hurry and
pick up your bag first. Then we'll go to my
house. Miss Trask says she has a special supper planned for us for tonight."

The girls ran up to the warm, delicious-
smelling Belden house. Trixie, filled with
glee, kissed everyone good-bye and col-
lected her weekend case.

"Now don't forget to help out Jim and
Brian," she said to Mart.

"I've never met anyone," Mart said, with
an admiring glance at his younger sister,
"who had quite the facility that you have for

getting out of chores! You've done it again. Every time I turn around, you have another new and exotic reason why I have to do the chores that you've signed up to do. You get all the credit, Miss Trixie Belden, and I get all the work!"

"Oh, Mart," Trixie said happily. "I'll make it up to you, I promise. Don't be jealous because I'm going to Paris."

"For your information, I am not jealous," Mart said, turning his head away. "It just so happens that when I go to Europe, I plan to go by myself on a tramp steamer. I think that's much more colorful, and more educational, too!"

"Sour grapes," Trixie said.

Mart gave her a little smile, as Trixie felt Bobby's small hand slip into hers.

"Trixie, forget about Mart," Bobby wheedled, as he snuggled up against her side. "Give me three more big kisses."

Trixie forgot about Mart, just as Bobby had asked, and gave her little brother some extra good-bye kisses and hugs.

"Okay, Bobby," she said at last. "Now you take good care of Reddy."

"And Moms, too," Bobby said solemnly.

The two girls were finally able to get out the door. They ran all the way along the foot-path to the Manor House. In a matter of hours they would be on the plane, winging their way to a whole new world!

6 * The Parisian Doll

TRIXIE ADJUSTED the pillow behind her head. She pulled the blanket up to her chin and tried not to listen to the excited beating of her heart. She could see through a crack in the curtain that separated the cockpit from the passenger section of the small plane. A warm blue glow emanated from the control panel, and the reassuring sight of the Wheelers' pilot, Bob Murphy, sitting at the controls helped Trixie settle down. The plane's engines hummed steadily.

Closing her eyes, she reviewed the evening's events and tried to feel a little bit sleepy. Honey and Trixie had eaten an elegant dinner with Mr. and Mrs. Wheeler. Later, they all sat around the roaring fire in the living room and discussed their plans for the trip.

Mrs. Wheeler was planning to attend a showing at one of the couturier houses Saturday afternoon. But Honey and Trixie weren't interested in fashion at all. At the sight of their crestfallen expressions, Mr. and Mrs. Wheeler decided that the girls could be on their own Saturday afternoon.

Trixie felt so grown-up she didn't even have the slightest desire to cheer when the driver came in to announce that the limousine was loaded and it was time to go.

At the airport, Trixie was amazed at the size of the Lear jet. From the outside it had looked small, but inside it was roomy and comfortable.

"Put your seat belts on," Mr. Wheeler said, as he settled in and lifted his briefcase to his lap. "I'm going to work for a little while, but I'll draw the curtain across the aisle so the light won't keep you up."

"You should both try to sleep," Mrs. Wheeler advised the girls fondly. "I know it might be difficult, but otherwise you'll feel simply awful tomorrow."

Trixie and Honey did as they were told, flipping off the overhead light switches. Trixie gazed out the small window at her side. The pavement seemed to move as the plane taxied out to the runway. They stopped for about four minutes, and then suddenly the engines went into high gear. The plane moved swiftly forward. Trixie felt just as if she were glued to the back of the seat as the small jet drove forward at incredible speed.

"We go about 180 miles an hour right before takeoff," said Mr. Wheeler. "That's pretty fast, isn't it?"

Trixie was about to comment, when suddenly the plane lifted off the ground. At that moment, she felt as if her stomach had stayed behind, but soon she was able to look down and see the twinkling lights of Westchester rapidly falling away below them. The plane banked gently, then flew straight as they gained altitude. After a while, Trixie could no longer see any lights below, and

she realized they were out over the ocean,
heading for France.

A slight jolting sensation pulled Trixie out
of her dreams. Thinking that her eyes had
been closed only for a second, she rubbed
them and tried to focus out the window. It
was daylight, and the plane had just touched
down. She saw a sign that said ORLY.

"Are we here already?" she asked. "Didn't
we just take off?"

Mr. Wheeler laughed heartily as he pulled
back the curtain that separated him and Mrs.
Wheeler from the two girls.

Mrs. Wheeler was just sitting back down.

"Why don't you girls freshen up in the
bathroom," Mrs. Wheeler said, smiling. "It's
right at the back of the cabin."

"You go first," Honey mumbled sleepily.
"I need more time to wake up."

Trixie emerged a few minutes later, feeling a good deal better. Her hair wouldn't be-
have at all the way it should, but Trixie
didn't mind. The plane taxied along the runway until it reached a small hangar. By the
time Honey had freshened up, the plane had
stopped and the passengers were ready to

get off. They went through customs, and Mr. Wheeler got them settled in a cab.

Trixie watched out the window in amazement as the taxi sped from the airport, taking them into the center of Paris. She gasped with delight as they passed by the Arc de Triomphe. It was even more beautiful than she'd imagined.

The taxi left them at the Hôtel Nova Parc Elysée. After Trixie and Honey had settled into the room they were to share, Mrs. Wheeler stuck her head through the doorway of the adjoining suite.

"Now, girls," she said, smiling at the pile of clothes yet to be hung up. "I'm off to Saint Laurent, but I've left word with the manager to get you a taxi. It will be at your disposal for the afternoon. You won't have to pay the driver, because the fee will go on the hotel bill. But here are some francs, just in case. You can buy snacks or whatever you'd like."

"Oh, thank you, Mom," Honey said, as she put the folded bills in her purse. "Will the taxi driver just wait for us while we're in the museum?"

"Yes, dear. I've asked them to find a driver

who speaks English," Mrs. Wheeler continued, "so you shouldn't have any problems. Now, have a nice day, and meet us back here by 6 o'clock at the latest."

"Okay, Mom," Honey said. She watched the door close behind her mother, then turned to Trixie. "We'd better turn our watches forward, or we'll never know what time it is."

"Good idea!" Trixie adjusted her watch, and then the two girls took the elevator down to the main lobby.

"Wait a minute, Honey," Trixie said, suddenly stopping. "What about Mr. Reid? Shouldn't we pick up the doll?"

"I was just thinking about that," Honey said, as they made their way through the glass doors in search of their taxi. "Let's pick up the doll first, and then go to the Louvre. We can ask the driver to take us to the address Mr. Reid gave us. I have it right here."

Trixie nodded in agreement, and then stood back as Honey asked the doorman to point out their taxi. The doorman led them to one of the black cabs that was parked a short distance away.

"Charles, these are the young ladies you

will be driving today," the doorman said. Charles smiled, and opened the door for his passengers.

"I am told I am to take you to the Louvre," he said haltingly.

"That's correct," Honey said. "But would you please take us to this address first?"

Handing the slip of paper to him, she waited as he examined it closely for a moment.

"We have to pick up a package," she explained, "and then we'll be going to the museum."

"Very well," Charles said, and the taxi started off through the streets of Paris.

As they crossed one of the many bridges over the Seine, several barges were making their way along the river. The smokestack of one barge was tilted back, allowing it to pass under the low bridge.

Soon the cab was heading through the winding back alleys of a very run-down part of the city. Small, weather-beaten buildings were sandwiched in between blank-faced warehouses and factories. Very few people were in the streets. This wasn't at all the kind of neighborhood Trixie had been ex-

pecting. It was so deserted! Trixie felt a sudden shiver of worry between her shoulder
blades.

Before she could voice her worries to
Honey, the cab pulled to a stop before a de-
crepit little shop. A crooked sign over the
door said EMILE FAURIER in faded letters.
The sidewalk in front was littered with
crumpled papers, and the store looked as if it
should have gone out of business years ago.
The windows were so encrusted with dirt
that it was impossible to see inside.

"Wait here," Honey said to Charles, and
the girls climbed out of the car. They cau-
tiously opened the rickety door. There was
no one inside, but soon a small, stooped man
wearing thick glasses emerged from the
back. Trixie could see a dusty display of
watches on the counter, but the rest of the
shop seemed to be empty.

"We're l-looking for André, please,"
Honey stammered. She handed the envelope containing the note across the cracked
glass of the counter. The man opened it and
peered at the note for what seemed like a
very long time.

At last he nodded briefly and went into the

back of the shop. In a few minutes he returned, carrying a large wooden box. Pulling a sheet of brown paper from somewhere under the counter, he quickly wrapped the box and tied it with an old piece of string. All this time, he spoke not a word. But when the package was wrapped, he handed it to Honey and flashed a toothless smile.

"Merci, mademoiselles," he said with a bit of a lisp, and then shuffled over to sit down in a rickety chair in the corner.

Honey held the box for a few moments, uncertain about what to do.

Then she murmured, "Thank you—I mean, you're welcome," and turned to leave.

Trixie held the door for her, and they stepped outside into the street.

"Wow," Trixie said. "That was the strangest thing I've ever seen. Who was that man anyway? Do you think he was André?"

"I don't know," Honey replied, shifting the box to her other arm. "I wonder what kind of shop that is?"

"Beats me," Trixie said. "Maybe it's a watch shop, but it looks to me as if they haven't sold a watch in twenty years!"

She stopped speaking as, from the corner

of her eye, she became aware of someone watching them. She turned and saw a tall, thin man with bushy red eyebrows standing in a doorway a few yards away. He was wearing a dingy trench coat and his hat was pushed back to reveal a shock of flaming red hair. Their eyes met and locked for a second. Then the man began to walk toward them.

"Quick, Honey," Trixie said. "Get in the taxi!"

Before Honey could protest, Trixie opened the taxi door and shoved her friend inside. Then, climbing in after her, she quickly slammed the door.

"Drive somewhere. Anywhere!" Trixie commanded Charles. She pushed down both locks. "And drive fast!"

"Something is wrong, mademoiselle?" asked Charles.

"No. We, uh, we're just in a hurry," Trixie replied.

"What is the matter with you?" Honey whispered.

"There was a strange-looking man out there," Trixie said, twisting so she could get a better view out the back window. "He was watching us."

"What's wrong with someone watching us?" Honey asked.

"He seemed too interested in us," Trixie said, frowning and thinking hard. "But maybe he was more interested in our package. Maybe he was going to steal it from us!"

"Do you really think so?" Honey gasped. "I think maybe we'd better take it back to the hotel before we go to the Louvre. After all, Mr. Reid said the doll was very valuable, so perhaps we shouldn't take any chances. Charles?"

"Yes, mademoiselle?"

"Would you mind taking us back to the hotel for a minute?" Honey asked. "We'd like to drop this package off before we go to the museum."

"Not at all, mademoiselle."

A few moments later the taxi pulled up in front of the reassuringly familiar building. Trixie and Honey dashed up in the elevator, carefully placed the box onto one of the beds, and then went back downstairs. They quickly climbed into the waiting taxi.

"That's finally settled," Honey said with a sigh. "Now let's get on with the sight-seeing!"

Charles put the cab in gear, and off they

sped. But Trixie couldn't stop thinking about the man outside the shop where they'd picked up the doll—if it really *was* a doll. *After all,* she thought, *we never saw what was in that box, did we?*

But the beautiful view out the window proved to be a much stronger attraction than any thoughts about the mysterious stranger and the peculiar shop. Soon the taxi pulled up in front of an enormous building.

"Here you are," said Charles. "The Musée du Louvre."

The girls spent all afternoon wandering from room to room, across centuries of art history. Overwhelmed by the beautiful paintings, elegant furniture, and imposing statues, they walked as if in a trance. They managed to see the Gothic and Renaissance collections, the tapestries, the medieval metalwork, and the Renaissance bronzes. At last, they began to slow down.

Honey glanced at her watch and sighed. "It's almost 5 o'clock," she said. "It will probably be closing time soon. We'd better go back to the hotel. I think I need to soak in a hot tub!"

Trixie agreed emphatically, and they dragged themselves back downstairs to find

Charles waiting for them in front. The girls sat in limp silence as Charles drove them back to the hotel. Mrs. Wheeler was there, very glad to see they had made it through their day in Paris safely.

"Rest for an hour before dinner," she suggested, when she saw how tired they looked.

Trixie took off her shoes, and put her weary feet up on the satin bedspread. But after lying quietly for a while, she abruptly sat up again.

"I'm going to open that box and take a look at this doll," she said firmly. She carried the package to her bed. "This thing is awfully heavy, Honey. Didn't you notice when you were carrying it?"

"It seemed fine to me. But maybe we shouldn't open it," Honey said, a worried expression on her face. "Mr. Reid specifically said not to take the doll out. If we open the box, we might not be able to get it closed correctly."

"Don't worry," Trixie said. "I'll be careful. Besides, I'm just going to look. I won't take her out. We'd better make sure we picked up a doll and not something else."

"Why would we get something else?" Honey asked, startled.

"I don't know," Trixie answered, as she untied the string and took off the plain brown paper. "Let's just say I have a feeling, that's all. What if the man made a mistake? We'd feel pretty silly if we went to all this trouble and didn't bring back the right package."

"I suppose you're right," Honey said as she watched Trixie slide the top off the wooden case.

"Gleeps, Honey!" said Trixie. "Take a look at this!"

Inside the case was the most beautiful antique doll the girls had ever seen. The doll was dressed in an exquisite, lavender satin gown, with a pale-blue front panel trimmed in lace.

"Golly," Trixie said. "She looks just like Marie Antoinette."

The delicate porcelain face had a rosebud mouth. The doll's blonde hair was piled high on her head, and a few fat ringlets fell to her porcelain shoulders. A little beaded purse dangled from her china wrist, and it was obvious to both girls that she was very valuable.

"No wonder Mr. Reid wanted to be extra

careful with this doll," Trixie said. "She's probably worth a fortune!"

"We'd better put her back now," Honey said. They carefully slid the top back on the wooden case and wrapped it up again.

Before they had a chance to discuss the doll any further, Mrs. Wheeler knocked on the connecting door.

"Start getting dressed, girls," she said. "We'll be going down to dinner in about fifteen minutes."

Trixie and Honey rushed to get ready. Gazing at her reflection in the mirror, Trixie was surprised to see that she looked presentable. Perhaps it was because she was in Paris, or maybe it was the fancy hotel. Trixie turned this way and that, pleased for once with her reflection.

The girls joined the Wheelers and had a delicious French dinner in the hotel dining room. After a rich dessert, they returned to their room, exhausted, and flopped into bed. As soon as their tired heads hit the fluffy pillows, they were fast asleep.

During the next two days, Honey and Trixie went on a whirlwind tour of Paris with Mr. and Mrs. Wheeler. On Sunday, they took a sight-seeing trip on the Seine in a glass-covered boat; they went to the top of the Eiffel Tower and got a spectacular view of Paris as the sun was setting; and they ate in a charming little Left Bank cafe.

On Monday, they went out to Versailles for a tour of the park, the gardens, and the palaces. Trixie was awed by the luxury and wealth of the former French kings. She began to feel a little like Marie Antoinette as she fell under the spell of the huge palace.

As they came out of the smaller palace, Petit Trianon, Trixie suddenly felt a shiver of warning travel up her spine. Whirling around, she could have sworn she saw the red-haired man.

She quickly scanned the crowds but he wasn't there. Unable to tell for certain whether she'd seen him or not, she finally decided it was just her imagination.

They returned to Paris, had an early dinner, and then taxied quietly out to the airport.

As they walked through the airport, Trixie again had the distinct feeling they were being followed. Whipping her head around, she caught sight of the man with the red hair and bushy eyebrows standing next to a newspaper vendor.

This time she was sure. The red hair, the rumpled trench coat, and those strange bushy eyebrows! But what was he doing here? Suddenly Trixie was certain that the man was following them. But why?

She quickly tugged on Honey's sleeve. Pulling her back a few paces behind the Wheelers, Trixie urgently whispered in her ear.

"Remember I told you someone was watching us when we picked up the doll?" she said. "Well, he's been following us, and he's back there by the news vendor! Take a look!"

Honey stopped and looked over her shoulder.

"Trixie, are you sure?" Honey asked, turning back. "I don't see anyone by the vendor."

"He's wearing a trench coat and has red hair and bushy eyebrows," Trixie whispered.

Honey didn't see anyone fitting that description. When Trixie turned around, she didn't see a trace of the man either.

"Hurry up, girls," Mrs. Wheeler called.
"We're about to board!"

Trixie took one last look around, but the
mysterious stranger had vanished.

In a matter of moments, they were climbing the metal steps to the plane. As Trixie
settled in and fastened her seat belt, she
wondered if perhaps she'd been wrong. But
in a few seconds, it wouldn't matter anyway.
They were leaving Paris and the strange red-
haired man behind.

7 * A Suspicious Stranger

Trixie slept right through the six-hour flight back to Westchester Airport. She was still drowsy when she went through customs. Because of the time difference, she was home in the cozy living room of Crabapple Farm by 7:30 Monday evening. She was so tired she almost fell asleep in the middle of reading Bobby his bedtime story. The next morning, however, she felt completely refreshed.

"Brian, do you think you could help us this afternoon?" Trixie asked at breakfast.

"Of course," Brian answered as he finished off his third piece of toast. "What can I do to help our new member of the jet set?"

"Well, the problem is that we have to bring Carl Reid the antique doll we picked up for him in Paris. But I don't think we should take it to school with us," Trixie explained. "I was sort of hoping you would drive us over there in the Bob-White station wagon this afternoon."

"Sure thing. I'll meet you two when you get off the school bus," Brian said. "But, just one question. Why did you do a favor for Mr. Reid? And who is Mr. Reid anyway?"

"Oh, Brian, you know who he is!" Trixie groaned. "He's the owner of that new antique store. He just asked us to pick up this doll while we were in Paris."

"Well, if you didn't mind picking it up," Brian said, "I don't mind dropping it off. It just seems like an odd thing to do on your weekend in Paris."

"It was no trouble at all," Trixie said airily. But she realized that she wanted to discuss the red-haired man with Brian. "I would like to talk to you about it later if you have some time, though."

"Problems?" Brian asked, suddenly con-cerned.

"Not really," Trixie answered, gazing at him fondly. "Just some questions, that's all."

Mart came into the kitchen.

"You guys are going to miss the bus, if you don't stop colloquializing," he reminded them.

"Oh, thanks for telling us," Trixie said. She grabbed her jacket and slipped it over her shoulders. She and Brian quickly col-lected their books and ran out the door. They all got to the end of the driveway just as the school bus rounded the corner.

During lunch, Trixie told Honey that Brian would drive them to The Antique Barn after school. Honey, who had put the pack-age in her closet, was delighted at the news.

"I was wondering how we'd get the doll to Mr. Reid without taking it to school first," she said, greatly relieved.

"Well, if it weren't for the Bob-White sta-tion wagon," Trixie said, "we'd really have a problem."

The bell rang, and babbling voices, scrap-ing chairs, and shuffling feet made further conversation next to impossible.

"See you on the bus," Trixie said, and she made her way to her next class.

True to his word, Brian met them with the station wagon when they got off the bus. They drove to the Manor House to get the doll, and then went on to The Antique Barn.

"I'll wait out here for you," Brian said, when they pulled into the small parking area by Mr. Reid's antique store. "I'd rather listen to the radio than a whole bunch of chit-chat about dollies."

Trixie laughed. "We're only going to be gone a minute."

Pleased at having accomplished their mission in Paris, Trixie and Honey walked sedately into The Antique Barn carrying the box.

Carl Reid immediately took it from them, and carried it to his desk without a word. Quickly ripping off the wrapping paper, he slid back the top. He reached inside and roughly pulled the doll out of the box. While Honey and Trixie watched in amazement, he sqeezed the doll's arms, torso, and dress. Then, with a satisfied smile, he set the doll down on his desk and turned to the girls.

"Is anything broken?" Honey asked, looking worried.

"Nope. And thank you very much," he said, smiling absently. "Now it's getting late, and I have lots to do."

"You're welcome, Mr. Reid," Trixie said. Then she stepped forward. "Actually, I have a sort of favor to ask you, too, if you have a minute."

Mr. Reid looked at her sharply. "Yes?"

"Uh, well," Trixie continued as quickly as possible, "I have this article to write for the school paper about a local merchant, and I wanted to write my article about you and the antique toys in this store. They're so interesting, and I'm sure everyone else would think so, too. And it would be helpful advertising for you if there was an article about your—"

"No articles!" Mr. Reid interrupted. "I mean, not this week. I have a lot of things to take care of—Christmas season, you know. Maybe after Christmas. Now look, I've got work to do. I'll talk with you two some other time."

Shocked at his response, Trixie could do nothing but mumble good-night and stalk out the door.

"Of all the nerve!" she snapped, as she got into the car. "After I did a favor for him, would he do one for me in return? No, he would not."

"What's all this about?" Brian asked, shutting off the radio and backing the car out onto the road.

"That selfish man won't even let me interview him for the school newspaper!" Trixie said, folding her arms across her chest in disgust. "After the big favor we did for him, I think that's crummy! I only want half an hour of his time. What nerve!"

Honey didn't have anything to say, and Brian drove them quietly home while Trixie fumed.

They pulled up in front of the Manor House, and Honey got out of the station wagon.

"See you tomorrow!" she called.

"Bye," Trixie said glumly. She didn't say a word as Brian parked the Bob-White station wagon, and then she stomped into the house.

Trixie tried to get up the stairs to her room where she could fume in privacy, but she was stopped by Bobby. The little boy came running around a corner and grabbed her knees.

"Trixie, Trixie, Trixie," he sang. "I'm so

glad you're home early! Could you please help me with my room?"

"Oh Bobby," Trixie said. "I have so much to do. Why do you need help?"

"Moms says I have to clean up my room," Bobby moaned. "She says I'll get lost in there one of these days, and no one will be able to find me!"

"It's true that you have a lot of junk," Trixie said, drawn out of her bad mood by Bobby's little worried face. "But I doubt if you'll get lost in there before this weekend. I promise I'll help you then, okay?"

"Okay," Bobby agreed. "But Moms says I have to clear a path to my bed right now. Could you help me just a little tonight?"

"All right, sweetie," Trixie said. "Just let me take off my jacket, okay? I'll help you until dinner time, but after that, I have a ton of homework to get done."

Even though Trixie was annoyed at Mr. Reid for not agreeing to the interview, it turned out for the best. She was so busy all week with chores and homework that she wouldn't have had time to do the interview anyway. She and Honey had not practiced their spelling words in Paris after all, and now they had to work twice as hard to catch up. The Eastern Regional was on Saturday. They practiced every chance they could find, but Trixie worried that it was not enough.

With high hopes, but rather low expectations, the two girls went into New York City on Saturday morning, accompanied by Miss Trask and Helen Belden. The spelling competition was held in one of the big conference rooms at the Sheraton Hotel. Trixie and Honey were so nervous when they were seated at the front of the large room filled with strangers, they could barely breathe. Trixie's plaid wool skirt felt even itchier than usual. It was all she could do to keep from squirming in her seat.

The voice of the competition leader seemed to be coming through water, and when it was Trixie's turn she felt strangely light-headed. She stood in front of the microphone, listening carefully.

"Miss Trixie Belden from Sleepyside-on-the-Hudson. The word is—*pusillanimous*."

Trixie's answers sounded to her as though they were being delivered by someone else, and she felt miles and miles away. The microphone had a strange echo to it. Afterward, Trixie had very little recollection of anything she had said, and no recollection of Honey's answers, either.

"Talk about stage fright," Honey said as they left the room.

"I really wasn't that keen on winning," Trixie said, punching the elevator button. They all stood waiting.

"Well, I'm glad you feel that way," Miss Trask said, with a somewhat pleased expression. "After all, winning isn't everything, you know."

"I know. It's how you play the game," Honey said. Honey always knew how to finish Miss Trask's sentences.

"Well, I thought you girls did very well," Helen Belden said, gazing at them with obvious pride. "Some of those words were terribly difficult!"

"Oh, Moms," Trixie said. "You're so sweet to feel that way. I'm sorry I lost, but, to tell you the truth, I'm sick of studying spelling words!"

"Me, too," Honey agreed. "I was beginning to dream spelling words! If we had won this contest, we would have had to spend the next six months saying things like 'iconoclastic' and 'discrepancy' to each other. I don't think I could have stood it!"

Trixie suddenly felt free. In the elevator, she and Honey could hardly keep from giggling. Finally, the doors slid open in the main lobby, and released them.

"Are you sure you don't have some odd form of claustrophobia?" Honey said, bursting into laughter. "You know, the kind that gives you hysterics in enclosed spaces?"

"Claustrophobia," said Trixie. "C-l-a-u—" Before she could finish, they fell against each other, laughing.

They made their way across the big lobby behind Mrs. Belden and Miss Trask. Trixie loved to look at people when she was in New York City. Their faces seemed so much more interesting than the ones she saw every day in Sleepyside.

She realized that it was probably just her own imagination that made it seem that way. But so what? She still liked to look at each person and try to figure out what sort of life they led. Perhaps they were movie stars, or maybe rich financiers, or even spies from foreign governments!

Suddenly, she was jolted out of her reverie by something far more upsetting than her own romantic imaginings. Her stomach contracted sharply as she caught sight of a familiar face in the lobby, and she grabbed Honey's arm for support.

"Honey!" she gasped, pointing toward a group of armchairs by the window. "He's right there! Look!"

"Who?" Honey asked.

"The red-haired man from Paris!" she managed to say. "He's sitting right there!"

Honey looked. Sure enough, there was a man with red hair sitting in the Sheraton lobby.

"But Trixie," she whispered. "Are you sure he's the same one you saw in Paris?"

"I'm positive," Trixie said. "What on earth is he doing here? I wonder if he saw us? Let's get out of here."

When Miss Trask asked the girls if they wanted to stop for ice cream sodas, she was mildly surprised that they turned down the offer and asked to be taken home. Miss Trask and Mrs. Belden glanced at each other, deciding that perhaps the girls were more upset about losing the Eastern Regional than they'd originally let on.

"All right then," Mrs. Belden said, smiling at them sympathetically. "I believe we can just make the 4:40 out of Grand Central if we rush."

"Yes," Trixie said, glancing over her shoulder. "That sounds like a terrific idea. Let's rush!"

Trixie practically dragged the two women through the street and onto the bus. It wasn't until they were all settled comfortably on the train to Sleepyside that she let out a sigh of relief.

"I kept my eyes peeled while we were walking," she whispered to Honey, "and I don't think he followed us."

Honey glanced around them nervously, but saw nothing out of the ordinary.

"Trixie," she finally said when Miss Trask and Mrs. Belden were involved in a conversation. "Are you really sure that man was the same one you saw in Paris?"

"I'm positive," Trixie said firmly. "Now, I just have to figure out why he's here!"

8 * Wrongly Accused

TRIXIE PUSHED through the crowds of students in the school cafeteria, and tossed her books down on the table. She squeezed in between Mart and Brian, and tried to catch her breath. All the other members of the Bob-Whites were there too, because Trixie specifically asked them to meet her that day.

Trixie had decided that it was time to discuss her problem with all the Bob-Whites. She knew she could count on their help in times of need. But since they all had such busy school schedules, it had been a couple of days before she could get them all together. Only Dan couldn't come today, because he was working.

"Sorry I'm late," she said.

"Typical," Mart said. "It's just like you, Trixie, to call an emergency meeting and then neglect to show up."

"But I did show up," Trixie retorted. "It's just that Mr. Stratton asked me to finish washing the beakers after chemistry, and I could hardly refuse, could I?"

"Okay, I have to admit you have a point," Mart said with a smile. "Now tell us what this meeting is about."

Trixie looked at Honey, and then began to talk.

"I realize this sounds farfetched," she said when she'd told them all that had happened, "but I think there's a definite connection between Mr. Reid's antique doll and the man who was following us in Paris. I can't figure it out all by myself, and I think we should get together and investigate as a team."

"Not that I'm arguing with you," Brian said, "but we should clarify a few things first. Why do you think the store in Paris was so suspicious? Mr. Reid must know people besides antique dealers. Perhaps his friendship with this André is entirely unconnected to business."

"I suppose . . ." Trixie said, her voice trailing off.

"But someone was definitely following them, don't you think?" asked Di. She hunched her shoulders and leaned forward. Her worried gaze never left Brian's face.

"Well, I was about to get to that," Brian said. "There is always room for coincidence, you know. Americans and Europeans travel back and forth across the ocean every day. Besides, the man never said anything to you, did he?"

"No," Trixie admitted. "But why was he everywhere we went?"

"Could it be that your hyperactive imagination made you think you saw the same red-haired man everywhere you went?" Mart asked reasonably. "For example, people often say that I remind them of a certain person." He smiled mischievously at Trixie. "Maybe you just saw someone who looked like the man."

Jim agreed with Mart. "It could be that,

since you were frightened by the man waiting outside the store in Paris, you thought you saw him everywhere else."

"I suppose it's possible," Trixie said, "but that still doesn't answer the doubts I have about Carl Reid."

"Well, until he does something really dreadful or illegal," said Jim, "I'm afraid we have no reason to suspect him of anything."

"Innocent until proven guilty," Mart put in. "One of the great tenets of American law."

"Trixie," Honey said quietly, "I did see the man you pointed out in New York, but I'd never seen him before that. Remember, you were the only one who saw him in Paris. Until someone else sees him following us, too, there's no way we can be sure we're actually being followed."

"I know you're right, guys," Trixie said disconsolately. "It's just that I was so sure!"

"Well, try not to worry about it," Brian reassured her. "And if you see anything else, come and tell me right away."

"All right, Brian," Trixie said. "I suppose I'd better eat before the lunch period is over, huh?"

"Don't worry, Trixie," Mart said, eyeing

her lunch hungrily. "Anything you can't fin-ish will be taken care of instantly by yours truly over here."

"I wasn't worried," Trixie said, laughing at the expression on Mart's face. "Maybe we should tell Moms to pack you a boxcar-sized lunch instead of that measly little lunch-boxful."

"I'm going to run up to the library," Honey said. "I have a few last notes to col-lect for my paper in English. But I'll see you later on the bus. We're going to help Mrs. De Keyser again this afternoon."

"Oh, thanks for reminding me, Honey," Trixie said. "I'll see you later."

Trixie finished her sandwich, and rushed to her math class, trying not to think about the red-haired Frenchman. But all through the math class he stayed in her mind.

After school, Trixie and Honey went to Mrs. De Keyser's. They helped make a kid-ney-bean-and-ham casserole, then went up-stairs to clean. While they tidied up, they talked.

"I think Mrs. De Keyser is feeling a little better," Trixie said. "There hasn't been as much to do here lately."

"Perhaps she's getting more used to doing

things with one arm," Honey said. "And it
probably doesn't hurt her as much as it did at
first."

Suddenly, they heard a cry of dismay from
downstairs. They quickly ran to the top of
the stairs, and saw Mrs. De Keyser standing
at the open front door, calling frantically.

"Willy! Willy, you naughty dog!" Her
voice was shrill with worry. "Willy, you
come back here this instant!"

"We'll bring him back," Trixie called
down, figuring out what had happened.

"Oh, I feel so careless for letting him out
like that," Mrs. De Keyser moaned. "I just
opened the door for a second to put that bas-
ket of gourds on the porch. Before I knew it,
that dog just dashed out between my feet."

"Don't worry," Honey said comfortingly.
"We'll bring him back."

"I'm afraid that he'll run into the road,"
Mrs. De Keyser said. "He doesn't know how
to cross the street the way some dogs do. I'm
so afraid he'll be hit by a car."

Trixie and Honey put on their jackets and
ran out in search of Willy. They searched all
of Mrs. De Keyser's property. They even

went into the woods and across the road, calling as they walked. But Willy was nowhere to be found.

Disconsolately, they trudged back to the house, crossing behind the antique shop as they went.

"Look at that," Trixie said, glancing at the back of the shop. "The bottom half of the Dutch door is open about a foot. That's odd."

"It is," Honey agreed. "Mr. Reid doesn't seem like the sort who would leave a door open like that."

"That's for sure," Trixie said, with a rueful smile. "If it were up to him, he wouldn't even leave the doors unlocked. A customer might come and try to ask him a question, or buy something—heaven forbid!"

"Maybe Willy's inside the shop," Honey said hopefully. She went over and called his name as loudly as she could. Then she called in a softer, more wheedling tone of voice. But no one answered, least of all Willy.

"Oh well," sighed Trixie. "I guess we'd better go back and tell Mrs. De Keyser the bad news."

They called a few more times, then

walked back to the house, feeling completely useless. Each dreaded telling Mrs.
De Keyser. But she took it fairly well.

"He's done this before," she said. "I suppose it's partly because he never gets to run
by himself. I should probably have a fence
built around the property. That way he could
go outside on his own. But it's just too expensive to even consider."

"Would you like us to look some more?"
Trixie asked helpfully.

"No," sighed Mrs. De Keyser. "It'll be getting dark soon, and Willy will probably come
home then. Perhaps you could just tie up
those newspapers and magazines for me."

Trixie and Honey tied up the papers in
neat bundles, carried them outside, and
stacked them by the garbage cans.

"It's a good thing it gets dark so early
these days," Trixie said as the light rapidly
faded. "Otherwise, Willy wouldn't have any
excuse to come home for hours."

No sooner were the words out of her
mouth, when she heard a triumphant yip
from the road. Then a cold, wet nose
bumped against her leg.

"Willy!" Trixie cried happily. She brushed

her hand across his wiry coat. "Oh, Willy, you're all covered with burrs! What have you been up to, you rascally pooch?"

Willy ran ahead of them when they opened the front door, and headed straight for his bed by the fireplace. He didn't look at all ashamed when Mrs. De Keyser scolded him, but when he saw the dog brush he looked truly crestfallen.

"He hates being brushed," Mrs. De Keyser said. "But perhaps this will teach him not to go running off again. Now hold still, Willy."

But Willy was having no part of her attempts at grooming. Because of her broken arm, Mrs. De Keyser finally had to ask Trixie and Honey to do it for her. After a good half-hour's work, Willy was finally presentable.

The girls walked home as quickly as they could.

"See you tomorrow," Honey said, as she left Trixie to walk up the driveway to the Manor House.

"Don't work too hard on that English paper," Trixie called. Then she started off toward Crabapple Farm. As she walked, she thought about the math test scheduled for tomorrow. She wondered whether there was any point in studying, since she hadn't understood a single word of today's lesson. Geometry was not one of her best subjects. She could hear the sound of Bobby's happy laughter coming from the house. She opened the door and went inside.

"Trixie!" called Bobby. "Come up to my room! I want to show you all my new stuff!"

"Oh, Bobby," said Trixie. "I thought we just cleaned up your room! Don't tell me you brought in a whole bunch of new junk!"

"It's not junk!" Bobby retorted. "And besides, after we cleaned up so nicely, there was lots more room in there for good stuff!"

"Dinner!" Helen Belden called from the kitchen. "And I need someone to finish setting the table. Where are all my helpers anyway? I feel like the Little Red Hen in here all by myself. No one wants to help me make supper, but they certainly want to help me eat it!"

"Sorry, Moms," Trixie called. "I'll be right there. I just want to hang up my jacket and wash up."

"All right, dear," Mrs. Belden answered. "But hurry. I'd like the table set before we sit down, not after we finish."

Trixie set the table, and after dinner it was her turn to do the dishes. It was Mart's turn to read Bobby his bedtime story, so Trixie got a chance to sit down with her pesky geometry problems—something she desperately needed to do. After getting Brian to explain isosceles and equilateral triangles for tomorrow's math test, she was finally able to get ready for bed.

The next day, Trixie caught up with Honey in the hall after their last-period class.

"Oh boy," she sighed. "That test was pretty bad. Sometimes I wish I didn't have to take math at all."

"Don't worry so much, Trixie," Honey said, with a smile. "You always think you've failed those tests, and somehow you always manage to pass."

"I know, I know," Trixie said as they slammed their lockers closed and walked out to catch the school bus. "But one of these days, I may be right. Then will I ever be in trouble!"

"Well, worry about that when it comes,"

Honey said. "You're doing fine now."

As they strolled along the broad walkway in front of the school, Trixie suddenly heard a loud voice call their names.

"Miss Belden! Miss Wheeler! I think we'd better have a talk, young ladies!"

Trixie spun around, and stood face to face with a very angry-looking Carl Reid.

"My goodness, Mr. Reid," she said, trying to smile despite the sinking feeling she had after seeing his expression. "What's the matter?"

"The French doll is missing, and I have reason to believe that you two stole it!" came the grating reply. He held a slip of paper out so she could see it clearly. "Does this look familiar to you?"

Amazed, Trixie saw that it was a hall pass from school.

"I found this hall pass with your name on it right outside the back door of my shop. That door was open, and the doll was gone. Your only mistake was leaving a perfect clue lying on the ground."

"B-But, Mr. Reid," Honey stammered. "We didn't take the doll!!"

"I don't have to listen to your lying excuses, you little thieves," Mr. Reid said angrily. "I know why you spent all that time hanging around my store! You just wanted to steal something, that's all!"

"We haven't seen the doll since we brought it to you last week!" Trixie protested, shocked at his accusation. "And yesterday we were looking for Mrs. De Keyser's dog near your store—that's when the pass must have fallen out of—"

"A likely story, girls!" the angry man snapped. "You wretched teen-agers are all alike! Just no good. And believe me, I am not fooled by your innocent act!"

"We'll help you find the doll, but, honestly, Mr. Reid, we didn't—"

"That's absolutely right, girls. You *will* help me find that doll, because you're the ones who stole it." Mr. Reid began to walk away. But before he'd gone more than two feet, he stopped and whirled back to them. "And I'm going to press charges against you if that doll isn't back in my hands by tomorrow afternoon. Do I make myself perfectly clear?"

And with that, he stormed off and got into his car. The engine roared to life, and then the Mercedes-Benz screeched out of the school parking lot.

Shocked, and unable to move, Trixie and Honey stood glued to the spot. Then Trixie realized that school buses were beginning to pull out, and they ran for the Glen Road bus. On the way home they tried to think of some way to clear themselves. Of course they hadn't stolen the doll, but they might not be able to prove it to Mr. Reid or to anyone else for that matter.

They got off the bus filled with dread.

"I'll call you later, okay?" mumbled Honey as she trudged up the driveway. "Maybe I'll think of something."

"Right," Trixie muttered. But she'd been racking her brains on the bus, and hadn't been able to think of a single thing.

She couldn't even figure out why Mr. Reid was so quick to accuse them of such a terrible crime. That pass—which must have dropped from her pocket—wasn't proof. She had been to his shop a number of times, and furthermore she was at Mrs. De Keyser's house every other day. Why, that pass could have fallen from her pocket on Mrs. De Keyser's property and been blown by the wind across the hedge!

Stealing? The very idea of it upset her. Why, she wouldn't even borrow a dime from someone without paying it back!

9 * The Clue in the Dress

TRIXIE FELT terribly depressed, and at dinner she could barely push the food around on her plate, much less eat any of it. Worried, Helen Belden finally asked her if she was feeling all right.

"I've never seen you look like this, Trixie," she said, resting her hand lightly on the worried girl's forehead. "Are you sick?"

Trixie broke down and burst into tears.

"Oh, Moms," she sobbed. "The most terrible thing has happened."

The whole story came pouring out as the

shocked Belden family listened in silence.

"Listen, Trixie," Brian finally interrupted. "You mustn't cry so hard. You know very well that no one would ever believe that you and Honey had stolen an antique doll."

"Oh, Brian," Trixie said, as the tears poured down her face. "But what if this time they do?"

"Now Trixie," Mr. Belden said reassuringly. "What Brian says is true. And I want you to calm down. Stop worrying for a minute or two. Perhaps you can remember something that would help Mr. Reid find his antique doll. Perhaps Mrs. De Keyser can be of some help, too. She might have noticed something peculiar."

All this time, as the entire Belden family was trying to calm Trixie, Bobby Belden had been sitting silently in his chair, looking glummer and glummer. While Trixie described how Mr. Reid had threatened to have the two of them locked up, Bobby slid so far down in his chair that only the top of his curly mop of hair could be seen. And finally, when he could bear it no longer, great gulping sobs were heard coming from the vicinity of his seat. But Bobby wasn't in it.

"Bobby!" Trixie said, when she heard the sobs. "What's the matter, honey? Where are you anyway?"

Bobby was finally located under the table.

"He probably got scared when he heard you were going to jail," Mart teased. But this remark only made Bobby cry harder.

After a great deal of coaxing, he was finally convinced to explain what was bothering him.

"Oh, Trixie," he sobbed, burying his head in her lap. "I don't want to go to jail! Please don't let them send me, Trixie. I didn't mean it, honest!"

"Didn't mean what, Bobby?" Trixie asked, completely confused.

The muffled sobs continued from her lap. "I didn't take the doll at all, even though it's in my room."

Trixie lifted the tear-streaked little face, and looked into Bobby's eyes. "The doll is in your room?"

"Yeessss!" came the loud and miserable response. "A little doggie came over yesterday while I was playing in the yard. It was the little doggie that took the doll, but he gave her to me. I didn't know. Honest, Trixie. I didn't know!"

Trixie suddenly burst out laughing.

"Willy!" she shrieked. "Of course! It was Willy!"

On further questioning, Bobby described the dog, and Trixie was able to figure out what happened. But first, she excused herself from the table and ran up to Bobby's room. There was the doll, sitting up in the corner of his closet, surrounded by a collection of old bottlecaps, spiders' eggs, pinecones, and rusty garden tools.

As soon as dinner was over, Trixie immediately called Honey and told her to come over right away. In a matter of minutes, a pale, panting Honey came bursting in the front door, and together they gazed at the antique doll.

"It's her all right," Trixie said. "Would you believe it? That sneaky Willy ran into The Antique Barn and snitched her, just the way he snitched the feather duster and the bag of carrots."

"And you know how Willy loves kids," Honey said. "He was probably delighted that he had something to give Bobby as a present."

"She looks as if he dragged her through every bramble patch between Mrs. De Key-

ser's house and Crabapple Farm, though,"
Trixie said. "I'm afraid she's in terrible
shape. Maybe we'd better wash her dress before we give her back. Mr. Reid will be furious if he sees her looking like this!"

"Good idea, Trixie," Honey said. "But
let's hurry. Maybe if we wash the dress right
now, it will be ready by tomorrow afternoon."

Trixie picked up the doll and quickly un-
did the snaps at the back of her dress. Slipping the doll's china arms out of the sleeves,
she eased the dress down over the yellowed
lace petticoats that were underneath.

Suddenly there was a loud clatter on the
floor, and a muffled yelp of pain.

"Ouch!" Trixie said, dropping the dress in
surprise. "Something heavy just fell on my
foot!"

She bent down to investigate, and came up
holding a flat rectangular object. It was made
of heavy metal.

"Where did that come from?" she muttered in irritation. But Honey already had
the answer.

"I know," she said, holding up the little
gown Trixie had dropped. "Take a look. It

fell out of this dress, and there's another one in here, too."

Trixie took the dress from Honey. Sure enough, two hidden pockets were sewn in the underside of the satin gown—and still inside one of them was another metal plate.

"So that's why the doll was so heavy," Trixie reasoned. "I wonder what these metal plates are for?"

As Trixie and Honey began to examine them, Brian happened to walk past.

"Brian," Trixie called from Bobby's room. "Come and take a look at this."

She handed Brian one of the mysterious pieces of metal and watched as he held it up close, then turned it over and over in his hands.

"This looks like an engraving for a twenty-dollar bill," he said.

"Oh, sure," Trixie said sarcastically. But her heart began to pound.

Honey smiled uneasily, but Brian was still frowning at the plate.

"What does the other one look like?" he asked.

Trixie picked up the other plate, and was about to give it to her brother. But instead

she carried it over to the bright light of the
lamp where she could scutinize it carefully.

"I think this one's a twenty-dollar bill,
too—but it looks slightly different. Hand me
the other one, will you?"

Examining the two of them together, she
suddenly had a feeling that these plates
were far more important than any of them realized. She carried them over to the mirror.
Holding both of them up so they were re-
flected in the mirror, she gasped in horror at
the unassailable conclusion.

"Brian!" she said. "These are counterfeiting plates!"

"Let me see."

"You see what I mean? These are backwards," she said. "Look in the mirror."

Brian and Honey looked at the reflection
of the two plates in the mirror.

"See?" Trixie repeated. "A printing plate
is the reverse of the image which ends up on
the paper. This one is the front of a twenty-
dollar bill, and this is the back. That could
mean only one thing."

"What?" asked Mart as he came into the
room. "Is the schoolgirl shamus about to
make a stupendous pronouncement? If that's

the case, I wouldn't want to miss this one for the world!" Plunking himself down in a chair, he leaned forward eagerly. "Well?"

Trixie was so engrossed in her thoughts she didn't pay any attention to his teasing.

"That's right," she said. "Only one thing —Carl Reid is a counterfeiter! He's going to use these plates to make phony twenty-dollar bills!"

There was a leaden silence in the room. Finally Brian spoke.

"Trixie," he said quietly, "I think you're right. But this time I'm afraid you've really bitten off more than you can chew."

"I know," Trixie said. "What do we do next?"

"I don't understand," Honey said. "Why has she bitten off more than she can chew?"

"Simple," answered Trixie. "You see, Carl Reid wants his doll back because of these plates. It's not a valuable doll, at least not to him. It's what's in the dress that's valuable to him—these plates. If we return the doll without the plates, he'll know we've discovered his secret."

"And if you return the doll *with* the plates," Mart said, "he might be able to tell that you've tampered with it, found the plates, and then he might want to—"

"Don't say it!" Honey said loudly.

"Just a minute," Brian said. "We have to think this thing through carefully. The possibility always exists that he doesn't know about the plates. He could want the doll because he's interested in antique toys. Perhaps someone else is using him to transport these things into the country."

Trixie quickly picked up on Brian's train of thought.

"You mean someone who knows about the plates, and the fact that they're inside the doll's dress, would then come to his shop and buy the doll?"

"That's one possibility," said Mart. "Or perhaps someone intends to steal it from him."

"Oh no," Honey cried. "At this very moment, some awful criminal might be watching us! We could all be in terrible danger. Shouldn't we tell the police?"

"That's the worst thing we could do right now," Trixie said. "No matter who the actual counterfeiter is, the finger of suspicion points straight at us!"

"But we didn't do anything," Mart said. "Therefore we have nothing to worry about."

"Not so, I'm afraid," Brian answered sadly.

"Brian's right," Trixie said. "Counterfeiting is a federal crime, and it carries very high penalties. And counterfeiters stand to make a lot of money. I suspect that they're not very nice if they think someone has gotten in their way."

"Or might turn them in," Brian added.

"Well, what can we do?" Honey asked. "It looks as if we're in trouble if we return the doll, and we're in trouble if we don't."

"I'll think of something," Trixie said. "But before we do anything, let's try and get this dress tidied up. If it looks neat and clean, we might be able to get away with pretending we don't know anything."

The girls went into the bathroom and washed out the little gown. Then they hung it carefully to dry in Trixie's room.

"Tomorrow we can iron it," Trixie said as Honey was leaving. "Maybe he won't be able to tell that anything happened to the doll. And perhaps by then I will have figured out what to do."

"I certainly hope so," said Honey. She shivered slightly as she stepped out onto the porch. "Think hard, okay?"

"Don't I always?" Trixie said. "Don't worry."

"That's all very nice to say, Trixie Belden," Honey said. "You're usually the biggest worrier of all." She walked quickly down the steps. "Maybe this time Brian is right. Maybe we did bite off more than we can chew."

"Oh my goodness," Trixie exclaimed suddenly. "I almost forgot! There's a meeting of the newspaper staff tomorrow after school. That's really going to mess everything up. Now we have to ask Moms to pick us up. We'll miss the school bus because of the meeting."

"Why don't we take our bikes tomorrow?" Honey suggested. "That way, we'll have them after school and we won't have to bother your mother."

"Okay," Trixie said. "I'll meet you at the end of the driveway tomorrow morning."

"Great," Honey said. She turned to go. "See you tomorrow, then—and keep thinking hard!"

"Right," Trixie said. "See you."

Honey quickly made her way along the path between the two houses, and Trixie went upstairs to her room. The doll's dress hanging in the corner sent a quiver of apprehension dancing down her spine.

10 * Caught!

THE NEWSPAPER staff meeting after school the next day lasted so long Trixie thought she would sprout grey hairs if they didn't hurry up and get it over with. Under ordinary circumstances, Trixie liked the staff meetings, but today she had so many things on her mind she just couldn't keep her attention on any of it.

"Holy cow!" she said, as they finally ran down the stairs and found their bicycles in the lockup by the side door of the building. "You'd think they had nothing better to do than talk about how much money Mrs. Doherty in the knitting shop plans to make this season!"

"That *is* the assignment, you know," Honey said. "What else should they talk about—the price of tea in Istanbul?"

Trixie burst out laughing.

"I do declare, Miz Wheeler," she teased, affecting a southern accent. "Y'all sound just like my brother Mart."

But Honey didn't laugh. She frowned slightly and straightened up.

"Have you figured out what we're going to do about the doll?" Honey asked.

"Yes," Trixie answered firmly. She wheeled her bike out onto the sidewalk, and climbed on. "We're going to go home, iron the dress, and make it look as perfect as we can. We'll put the plates back inside, and return the doll. And we might just as well tell the truth. We'll say that my little brother found the doll in the yard."

"You mean we'll accuse Bobby?" Honey gasped.

"Of course not!" Trixie said. "It doesn't matter what we say, because I'm sure he won't believe us. I'll just tell the truth because it's no more believable than anything else we could think up. Mr. Reid won't care what we say. He wants that doll back very badly."

"You're right about that," Honey said ruefully.

"Besides, I can't imagine that he'd have us arrested for stealing a doll that was back in his possession," Trixie said. "And he can't very well call the police and tell them we stole a doll that just happened to have counterfeiting plates inside, can he? If he did that, then he'd have to be crazy."

"Or innocent," Honey put in. Because it was getting late and cold, they pedaled along Glen Road as quickly as they could.

"I'm not so sure he's innocent," Trixie said through clenched teeth. "Brrr. It's awfully cold out. I'm afraid it's time for us to put our bikes away for the winter."

They pedaled along in silence for a while, putting all their attention and energy into getting into a nice warm house. The wind had shifted and was now coming at them head on. Trixie's eyes were beginning to tear. Raising her hand, she brushed away a tear that was blurring her vision, and the bike swerved slightly. As it swerved she noticed, out of the corner of her eye, a blue sedan moving slowly behind them.

"Pull over onto the shoulder, Honey," she called ahead. "There's a car that wants to pass."

Trixie and Honey pulled their bikes over to the side of the road. They went slowly, waiting for the car to pass. But the car stayed where it was, a short distance behind them. Trixie began to get annoyed because it was harder and slower pedaling off the smooth pavement. The dry grass was bumpy, and the pebbles slippery.

"Well, why doesn't he go by?" Honey yelled. "We'll never get home at this rate."

But Trixie didn't answer. She was thinking. She slowed down a bit more and turned her head, trying to see the driver. And what she saw confirmed her worst fears. Her heart thudded. She speeded up until she was riding right alongside of Honey.

"Don't look now," she warned, "but it's the red-haired man from Paris! He's following us!"

"What!" Honey gasped. "What do we do now? There's no way we can ditch him on these bikes!"

"Yes there is. Now listen a minute. We just

passed the Glen Road Inn, right? You know that trail that goes through the woods and lets out a little past my house on Glen Road? We're going to try and get on it. He can't follow us in the car, and we might be able to get away. Now, follow me, and ride as fast as you can!"

Trixie set off with a furious burst of speed. She rode the bike back onto the pavement, and pedaled hard. She knew she would soon see a slight thinning of the trees. She hoped against hope they could maneuver their bikes through the low underbrush and pick up the path. It was the only way to lose him!

In order to catch them, their follower would have to pull his car off the road and go on foot through unfamiliar woods. Trixie knew the trail like the back of her hand, but a stranger would have difficulty following it—especially at night.

Suddenly, Trixie hit a patch of gravel on the road, and the bike skidded. Trixie managed to right it, but not before it swerved and wobbled onto the shoulder. Honey, who was right behind her, tried to avoid Trixie but failed. With a sickening crunch, the two of them went down onto the grassy shoulder in a spinning pile of bicycle wheels, arms, legs, and school books.

Trixie closed her eyes for a moment and prayed that the blue sedan would pass them. But her heart sank as she heard the sound of tires on gravel. The car pulled to a stop right in front of them, cutting off any escape.

Trixie untangled herself as quickly as she could and stood up. She didn't want to be lying in a heap when this strange man, whoever he was, came over to them.

"Stand up, quick!" she told Honey. "We can still run if we have to!"

Honey pulled herself out from under her bike, and the two of them watched as the door of the sedan swung open. A small pile of papers dropped out onto the ground and was immediately followed by two long legs.

The red-haired man uncoiled himself slowly from behind the wheel, and staggered out onto the road. He was still wearing the rumpled trench coat. He walked slowly toward them. His craggy face was set in a very disagreeable expression, and he didn't look as though he had anything pleasant to say either.

Scowling, the man stopped when he got

directly in front of them. With a flourish, he
pulled off his hat and nodded his head.

"Mademoiselles," he said. His voice was
rather high-pitched, and Trixie had the over-
whelming urge to giggle. "Mademoiselles, I
am Inspector Marcel Patou of the Paris
Sûreté, and I arrest you in the name of the
French authorities!"

"What?" Trixie and Honey said together,
astounded. "Arrest?"

This was the second time in little more
than twenty-four hours that someone was
threatening them with arrest—and they
hadn't done a thing!

"That is correct," the man continued. He
reached into the inside pocket of his coat
with an exaggerated motion. As he pulled
out a shiny badge, his handkerchief and a
notebook fell to the ground. When he bent
down to retrieve the items that had fallen,
his hat dropped to the ground as well.

"My identification," Inspector Patou said,
extending the badge in their direction. At
the same time he was trying to juggle his hat,
pen, and notebook—and doing a poor job of
it.

Trixie took the badge and peered at it in

the dying light. It certainly looked authentic, and she handed it to Honey. Honey's hand trembled as she took it. After looking at it briefly, she handed it back.

At that moment, Inspector Patou sneezed loudly, and the badge dropped to the ground between them. Trixie couldn't control the laugh that bubbled up inside her chest as she quickly stooped to get it.

She cleared her throat and tried to sound grown-up as she handed the badge back to him. "You are obviously who you say you are, but you have the wrong people, Inspector. By the way, you've neglected to tell us what we are being arrested for."

"Trixie!" Honey gasped in dismay. Honey would never have spoken that way to an adult. She was amazed at Trixie.

"You are under arrest for counterfeiting, of course," the French policeman answered. He wiped his brow with the rumpled handkerchief, then put it in his pocket. "I have been following you two young ladies since you made the pickup in Paris. You stopped at a shop called Emile Faurier—of this you are already aware—and took a package from a man named André. It is this package about which I am now speaking."

He stopped and carefully watched the expressions on the two faces before him.

"Yes, I can see that you know of which I speak," he continued, satisfied with himself. "Now then, young ladies, that particular shop has been under surveillance for a year, and we of the Sûreté know it is an outlet—as you say—for very high quality engravings used in making the currencies of many different countries. Since you and I both know that you picked up the plates, you might just as well tell me where they are now, and we will be finished with all this conversation."

He folded his arms across his chest, waiting for a reply.

"We didn't pick up any plates, sir," Trixie said, feeling a little frightened. "We picked up an antique doll. That was what was inside the box."

It had dawned on Trixie that they might still be in a lot of hot water. It would be one thing if the doll wasn't in their possession. Unfortunately, however, it was sitting at home on her dressing table. And the two miserable plates were sitting right next to it! If this detective followed them home, he would find the doll and naturally think them guilty.

"I do not believe you, I am afraid," he said, with a condescending smile. "How do two young ladies like yourselves get a ride to and from Paris in a Lear jet, eh? It smells to me of dirty money, mademoiselles, dirty money!"

"Now wait a minute!" Honey snapped angrily. "That plane belongs to my father! It has absolutely nothing to do with dirty money, and I won't let you say things like that about my father!"

"Aha!" Inspector Patou said, whipping out his notebook and pencil. Another shower of little papers fell to the ground at his feet, as he quickly scribbled something down. "So it is your father who is the counterfeiter, eh?"

Honey stamped her foot in vexation, but Trixie began to speak quietly.

"Excuse me, Inspector," she said calmly, "but I think I can help you. We picked up the doll at the request of a local antique dealer. He wanted us to carry it personally so it wouldn't get broken. However, the man is new in this area, and a very suspicious character in my opinion."

"In your opinion?" Marcel Patou's eyebrows shot up, and he watched her speculatively.

"And not only that," she continued, "I think he's your counterfeiter. I just remembered that he has an old printing press in the back of his store. I saw it there just a week or so ago. I'll bet he uses it to print the money!"

"The guilty are always 'just remembering' something that will cast one's suspicions somewhere else," Inspector Patou said smugly. "A press is not enough to prove a man's guilt. However, I must admit it is far more likely, this story you have told me, than that you two young ladies are part of a counterfeiting ring."

Trixie heaved a sigh of relief when she heard his words.

"And you say you have delivered the doll to this man?" asked Marcel Patou.

"That's correct," Trixie said firmly. She jabbed Honey in the ribs as she heard her sharp intake of breath. After all, she hadn't exactly lied, had she? They did indeed deliver the doll to Carl Reid. Marcel Patou hadn't asked them if they had somehow gotten it back, so she didn't have to mention it.

Besides, Trixie had a plan—a plan that would work much better if the doll were in her possession, not the Inspector's.

"And where is the antique shop?" he inquired.

"Right up this road, which is called Glen Road, by the way," Trixie answered helpfully. She wanted Inspector Patou to go away—and soon. "The name of the shop is The Antique Barn. You shouldn't have any trouble finding it."

"Very well, young ladies," he said. "I will investigate this matter. And if I need to speak with you again, I know where to find you . . ."

Letting his voice trail off in what Trixie decided was his "threatening" manner, Marcel Patou turned away abruptly and strode to his car. As he pulled open the door, he stumbled over a root and leaned heavily on the steering wheel. The horn blared loudly for a second or two before he managed to regain his balance and pull himself inside. He drove off, with a corner of his trench coat sticking out of the door and dragging along the road.

Trixie burst out laughing as he disap-

peared around the curve. Then she went
over and picked up her bike.

"Why didn't you tell him we have the
doll?" Honey asked, getting her bike too.

"Because I have a plan," Trixie answered.
"I'll tell you about it tonight at the clubhouse. I'll ask the other Bob-Whites to come,
too. Make it for 7:15, okay?"

"Okay."

Trixie started pedaling for home. Honey
followed behind her, wondering what on
earth Trixie had in mind.

11 * Trixie's Plan

AFTER DINNER, the Bob-Whites met in the clubhouse.

"It's absolutely freezing in here, Trixie," Mart said, rubbing his hands together briskly. "Why do we have to meet here? It's not as if we're lacking for warm places to meet, you know."

"You'll understand in a little while," Trixie told him. Turning to the rest of the group, she said, "I hope you all remembered to tell your parents we were going to the movie in town."

"I did," Di answered.

"Good," Trixie said, as all the other Bob-Whites nodded in the affirmative. The entire group—Di, Honey, Jim, Brian, Mart, and Dan—were dressed as if they were on an Arctic expedition.

"I must admit," Jim said with a smile, "I got some odd stares leaving the house in this outfit. Although I'm glad you told me to dress warmly, it looks pretty funny when you've just said that you're planning a nice evening in a heated theater."

"Sorry about that, folks," Trixie said, "but it's the only way. We'll be spending a little time sitting around in the dark in the woods."

"Okay, little sister," said Brian. "Enough of this mystery. Just what are your plans for the evening?"

"Well," Trixie said, pointing behind her. "In that paper bag is the doll. Honey and I washed her dress and ironed it. We put the plates back inside the dress exactly the way they were. Now I want to return the doll secretly to Mr. Reid."

"And how do you plan to accomplish this feat?" Mart said loftily.

"Easy," Trixie answered with confidence.

"We'll sneak up to The Antique Barn, put the bag on the doorstep, bang on the door— and then run like anything!"

"Then what?" asked Dan Mangan. He had arrived at the clubhouse a bit early, and Trixie had filled him in on everything that had happened so far. Dan knew now exactly how deeply involved they were. "You know," he said, "just giving the doll back doesn't solve anything."

"It may, and it may not," Trixie said. But she realized Dan was right. Her plan would work only if Carl Reid did exactly what she wanted him to do—and there was no way to make certain he would play his part. "We'll wait, and we'll watch. And if nothing happens tonight, we'll just have to keep on waiting and watching until something does."

Mart groaned so loudly it made Di jump.

"Mart!" she scolded. "Anyone listening to you would think someone had stuck a pin in your leg. Try to act in a civilized way."

Mart harrumphed, and the rest of the Bob-Whites laughed. But Brian immediately became serious again.

"Why don't we call the police?" Brian asked sternly. "I've been giving it a lot of thought and I still say you've bitten off more than you can chew. Counterfeiters have a great deal at stake. It might be extremely unwise for us to get any more involved than we already are."

"Not to mention unhealthy," Mart said. He was starting to pace back and forth. "It is my humble opinion that, just this once, we should let Sergeant Molinson of the Sleepyside police do his job."

"Sergeant Molinson would only put Carl Reid on the defensive," Trixie said. "Mr. Reid would never do something incriminating if he thought for one minute a policeman was watching!"

"The girl has a point," Mart conceded.

The rest of the Bob-Whites nodded in assent.

"Well," Brian said glumly, "if there's no other way, then we might as well get on with Trixie's plan."

Gloomily, the group left the safety of their clubhouse. Skirting the edge of the woods, they made their way along Glen Road. They didn't want to be seen, so it was impossible to take the station wagon. Driving a car up to the antique store would hardly be secretive.

After a brisk, half-hour's walk, they could see the lights of Mrs. De Keyser's house around the bend. Trixie had a difficult moment until she saw that lights were on in The Antique Barn, too. She also saw two long, black Cadillacs parked near the Mercedes-Benz.

"Whew," she whistled softly. "That's a break. The whole plan might have been ruined if Mr. Reid wasn't there."

She motioned the rest of the kids to stand in the shadow of the hedge. No sooner had they all gathered in the chilly dark than a familiar voice was heard speaking—practically in Trixie's ear!

"Good evening, mademoiselle," Marcel Patou said. "And to what do I owe this honor?"

Trixie almost jumped out of her skin.

"Is he the French policeman you were telling us about?" Brian asked, as he quickly came and stood next to her protectively.

Rapidly collecting herself, Trixie introduced Inspector Patou to the rest of the Bob-Whites. Then she explained what they were doing.

"Oh, Inspector," she said, as quietly as she could manage, "I'm afraid I wasn't entirely frank with you this afternoon."

"This is as I suspected," he responded

with a tight little smile. "And what exactly did you leave out, mademoiselle?"

"Er," Trixie stammered, "just one little thing. You see, actually we had the doll at my house. A little dog who lives in the house next door to the antique shop took the doll and gave it to my little brother. Then we, um, discovered these interesting things inside the doll's dress."

"What sort of interesting things, if I may ask?" Inspector Patou said.

"Well," Trixie continued bravely, "I guess they were, um, counterfeiting plates for twenty-dollar bills."

"And you have these counterfeiting plates with you now?" Marcel asked, his voice suddenly getting even more high-pitched than usual.

"Yes," Honey said quickly. "But we can't show them to you because we had to sew them back inside the doll's dress. If we take them out, Mr. Reid will know we've tampered with the doll and then . . ."

"I understand perfectly," he responded calmly. "And you have now come to return the doll, right?"

"Right," Trixie said. "We want to watch

and see whether Mr. Reid incriminates himself in some way."

"Very clever," the Frenchman conceded. "Dangerous, but clever. At least now I am here to help you."

Trixie really didn't see how the Inspector could help, but she finished explaining her plan. He agreed, and the Bob-Whites stationed themselves along the hedge. They stayed outside the circle of light around the shop, and watched silently as Trixie tiptoed to the door and quietly placed the paper bag containing the doll right in front. Before she could knock, though, Mart materialized at her elbow. "Too dangerous," he whispered, then tugged her away from the building.

Once they were back in the shadows, Trixie blew up. "What's the matter with you?" she snapped angrily. "I have to let them know that the doll is out there, don't I? Now let go of me, so I can knock on the door."

"Don't worry, Trixie," Mart said. "Have some faith in your smarter sibling. Let me handle this, okay?"

Trixie fumed, but stayed put, as Mart sneaked over to the driveway. He picked up a handful of pebbles, then backed into the shadows again. Taking careful aim, he tossed the handful of little rocks at the glass window.

Within a few moments, the door was flung open and Mr. Reid appeared silhouetted in the light.

"Who's there?" he said loudly, seeing no one and taking a step out onto the landing. At this moment his foot knocked against the paper bag. "What the . . . "

He picked it up, ripped open the paper, and pulled out the doll. Then he began to laugh.

"Hey, Bill, get a load of this! Those thieving little teen-agers returned our dolly," he called behind him. "Yeah, yeah. I'm gonna check and see if the contents are still there."

They could easily make out the way he squeezed the doll's satin skirt. Then they heard a relieved laugh.

"It's all here, Bill," he called inside. "All here."

Then the door slammed behind him, and once more it was silent outside. Trixie shivered slightly and whispered to Brian, who was crouching next to her.

"Now comes the boring part."

But the boring part didn't last too long. Shortly the door of the shop opened again, and three men came outside. The observers could see the mist of their breath against the light shining through the door. They opened the trunks of both Cadillacs and started unloading cartons.

"Let's get moving," one of the men said. It was Carl Reid. "We have to bring in this paper and we don't have all night."

"I hate this cold weather. Why didn't you set up this operation in Florida like I told you?" said one of the other men.

"They were on to us, that's why," Carl Reid said. "Now quit your noise and start unloading. Those stupid kids threw off our entire schedule."

"Yeah, yeah. We should have started printing yesterday. But who cares?"

"Louie cares, that's who. The pickup men have been waiting since yesterday."

The Bob-Whites listened, stunned. Trixie, even though this was exactly what she'd suspected, was suddenly amazed at being right. And rather frightened. All along, she had half hoped Mr. Reid wasn't involved, or that it was all an accident of some kind. Deep inside she had hoped that the plates had been hidden in the doll's dress for years—unbeknownst to Mr. Reid or even to André. But apparently that was not the case. Not only was Mr. Reid involved, but so was she—and so were the other Bob-Whites.

Inspector Patou held his finger to his lips, and everyone stayed quietly in the shadows and waited. It felt like hours to Trixie, and her feet were numb with the cold. Just when she thought she wouldn't be able to stand it another minute, the Inspector tapped her on the shoulder.

"It has been about forty-five minutes," he whispered, "and judging from the sounds I hear, I think the time has come for me to make my move, as they say."

"Good," Trixie whispered. "We're right with you."

"No, no, mademoiselle," Marcel replied. "This is no place for children. It is best for you to stay behind, thank you very much. I have only to catch him with the money, and my case is solved. But this could be a very dangerous moment."

He held up his hand to the rest of the Bob-

Whites, gesturing for them to stay behind. Crouching, he silently crossed the space separating them from the shop. Then, looking a great deal like a large scarecrow who had gotten off his pole in the farmer's field, he climbed the steps and kicked open the door.

12 * No Escape

CROUCHED in the dark by the hedge, Trixie watched the Inspector's gangling frame become silhouetted in the light of the door. Then, as if pulled by invisible strings, she stood up and began to run after him. She could hear the comforting sound of twelve feet scuffling behind her through the gravel, as the rest of the Bob-Whites followed her lead.

Without thinking about what she was doing, or why, she took the front steps of The Antique Barn two at a time and burst in right behind the Inspector. As her eyes adjusted to the bright light inside, she gasped.

Sitting on top of a round, antique oak table were six or seven neat stacks of freshly printed money. An open suitcase sat on the table next to the stacks. Through the door that opened into the back she caught a glimpse of the antique press. A square sheet of paper rested on its bed, and off to one side stood a man who was slicing rows of bills apart.

Everything seemed to move in slow motion as the three heads came up, and their jaws simultaneously dropped.

"What the . . ." Carl Reid growled, when he saw the intruders.

The other two men stopped what they were doing and came toward the group standing in the doorway.

Inspector Patou stepped forward quickly, separating himself from the Bob-Whites. He reached into his breast pocket and started to pull something out. Thinking he was reaching for a gun, the three men put their hands in the air.

"My name is Marcel Patou, and I am sent here from the Paris Sûreté to put you under arrest," he said, his voice rising shrilly. He whipped out the badge and identification papers from his inside pocket. When the men realized that he held only papers and no gun, their hands came down.

As the Inspector thrust the identification at them, the papers leapt from his hand and fell to the floor.

"Hey, boss," one of the men said. "This one's a tough guy. I'm scared, ain't you?"

But Carl Reid wasn't amused. "You can't arrest me, you dumb cop," he snarled menacingly. He headed toward the Inspector, who was bent over, retrieving his badge. "This is the United States, and you haven't got any jurisdiction here. You can't touch me."

Inspector Patou stood up, with an expression of shock and outrage on his face. Slowly, his frown deepened and the creases on his forehead resembled etchings in stone.

"I most certainly can arrest you, sir," he said slowly. "Since we are dealing here with the American dollars, I believe the American authorities will be more than happy to take you into custody. They will handle the formalities once I have turned you in. I think that perhaps your involvement with certain French criminals will make the remainder of my job much easier once I have returned to my country."

He drew himself up to full height and glowered at the smirking faces of the men who stood in front of him.

"Just one question, Frenchie," Carl Reid sneered. "Have you got a gun?"

As Carl Reid spoke, he reached inside his jacket and pulled out a nasty-looking revolver. The Inspector hesitated a moment too long and, before he could get his gun out, all three men were pointing guns at the little group standing in the doorway.

"Gimme the gun, Frenchie!" Carl Reid said icily.

The Inspector slowly, reluctantly, handed over his gun and then raised his hands over his head. His expression was one of resignation and defeat, and the Bob-Whites were stunned. They had set out to trap some counterfeiters—and they were trapped instead!

"Tie these jerks up," Carl Reid said wearily, gesturing at them with his thumb.

"We'll take care of them later—on the ride to Philly."

"Good idea, boss. You want me to put gags on them?"

"No," Carl Reid said after a short silence. "Unless, of course, they get noisy."

He and one accomplice kept their guns trained on the little group as the third man tied them up. Afraid to say anything, all that the Bob-Whites could do was look at each other in dismay. Brian caught Trixie's eye, but she was unable to read his expression. Di looked as if she was about to cry as the man approached her with the rope.

Appalled, Trixie watched as, one after another, the man tied them up. First he tied their wrists together, and then wrapped the remaining rope around their torsos, pinning their arms against their sides.

The group was powerless to prevent it from happening. Trixie desperately tried to think of something, but with two guns aimed at them, there was no alternative but to act docile.

Trixie's mind raced. *There has to be a way out of this*, she thought, trying to concentrate. *There are more of us than there are of them. But they have guns, and they're tying us up. Well, they haven't tied me up yet. I still have time to think of something.*

Then suddenly she did—and it was so funny she almost burst out laughing. *Lady! Of course! I'll do what Lady does!* Lady was one of the Wheelers' horses who was very clever. She also knew exactly how to handle people. Whenever she was saddled, she "blew herself up" to a larger size. Then she "let herself out." Naturally, a loose cinch meant the saddle would suddenly swing down to dangle loosely under her belly as soon as anyone tried to mount. You could almost hear Lady laugh each time she'd managed to fool someone. *I'll just blow myself up*, Trixie thought, *when he ties the rope around me. Then when I let myself out, the rope will loosen up just the way Lady's cinch does!*

At last the man came over to her. She carefully watched his face as he jerked her arms in front of her and prepared to loop the rope over her wrists. *If I can get untied*, she thought, *I can untie the others. Then maybe we can overpower them.*

She decided to give it a try. She clenched

her fists and twisted her wrists slightly as the rope looped over them. If she could somehow keep the ropes loose, then there was an outside chance she could wriggle loose when no one was watching. But the man pulled the ropes painfully tight and, with a sinking feeling, Trixie despaired of ever getting loose.

She hunched her shoulders and silently inhaled, filling her lungs with air as he pulled the rope down over her shoulders, pinning her arms against her sides. *I feel exactly like Lady*, she thought, as the rope pulled tight around her body, but she kept herself blown up. She desperately hoped she could hold her breath till he was through.

As soon as he had finished, she relaxed slightly and exhaled. However, she kept her muscles clenched just enough so no one would see the ropes slackening.

"Now sit down on the floor!" Carl Reid commanded, once they were tied up to his satisfaction. "And no tricks!"

Knowing the intruders were no longer able to interrupt, the three men quickly went back to work. From where they were sitting, the Bob-Whites could see the press in the back room. They watched glumly as the sheets of paper were fed into the press. The man running the press handed the sheets to the other man, who hung them up to dry. It was his job also to slice the dry bills apart. Mr. Reid counted and stacked the finished money.

Suddenly Trixie felt a nudge at her back. It was Honey.

"Maybe we should start screaming," Honey whispered in Trixie's ear. "Maybe Mrs. De Keyser will hear us."

"No," Trixie whispered back. "It's late, and she's probably asleep. We can't risk the chance that they'd gag us. I have a plan anyway."

When Trixie was satisfied that the three men were totally engrossed in their work, she started to wriggle ever so slightly. To her delight, she felt the ropes slowly slip. At the same time, she worked her wrists back and forth, trying to open up more slack. Working quietly for about fifteen minutes, she was finally able to get one hand free.

With a glance of warning at the others, she slowly began to shift her position toward Inspector Patou. Each time Carl Reid walked by with a stack of money, Trixie stopped moving, but at last she reached her goal.

Making as little noise as possible, she started to work on the knot behind the Inspector's back.

But trying to untie a thick knot with one hand was harder than Trixie had figured. *Now I know how Mrs. De Keyser feels*, she thought. *This is going to take forever, and I don't have forever. These guys are almost finished, and then we'll be completely up the creek!*

She was working the knot feverishly, when she caught sight of Mart's face. He was watching her intently. He gestured with his head to the door behind him.

What's he trying to tell me? Trixie thought, staring back at him just as intently. Then suddenly she knew! *He wants me to go for help! If I can just make it out the door without anyone noticing, I can get the police! Of course! There are so many of us in this little room full of junk, they might not notice if one of us disappeared.*

Slowly and quietly, Trixie wriggled her way to the door. Moving inch by inch, she kept her eyes trained on the three men in the back room. Carl Reid was the only one who came into the front part of the shop.

At last, she was within reach of the door-knob. At a moment when Carl Reid was safely in the back room, she quietly turned the knob until she felt the bolt disengage from the door jamb. Then she pushed gently on the door, hoping it wouldn't squeak.

Luckily the door was quiet. Trixie kept her eye on Carl Reid, knowing that at any moment he would return with a new stack of bills to be banded and put in the suitcase. She decided to wait until his next trip into the back room before making her escape.

As Trixie expected, Carl Reid came into the front of the shop. He stopped for a moment after placing the bills on the table. He looked at the silent group as if realizing there was something different about them. Trixie held her breath. Unable to determine what was bothering him, he returned to the back room.

Trixie watched until she was certain all three men were engrossed in their tasks. Then she pushed the door a little further open and slid as quickly as she could out onto the landing. Her heart pounded wildly

and, as she stood up, the ropes fell around
her feet.

In an instant, she heard a howl of rage. Before she could disentangle her feet from the
ropes, Carl Reid was at the door. His arm
shot out and grabbed her jacket. Trixie tried
to pull her arms out of the sleeves, but failed,
and Reid dragged her back into the shop.

"So, you thought you could run off and call
the cops or something, eh, kid? Well, that
was a big mistake, if you don't mind my telling you." He pushed her back down into a
sitting position, far away from the others.

"This time, I'll tie you up myself," he said
icily, shooting a disdainful glance in Bill's
direction. "And, believe me, you won't get
out of it because I know a thing or two about
tying someone up."

Trixie saw Mart giving her a sympathetic
look. He shrugged slightly, as if to say, "At
least you tried!"

Better to have tried and failed, she
thought, *than never to have tried at all*.

But Trixie had to admit Mr. Reid could
certainly tie a tight knot. Not only that, he
had tied her wrists behind her back instead
of in front, and the ropes bit into her wrists

and upper arms painfully.

Di started to cry softly. Hearing her, Brian had a look of barely controlled fury on his face as he watched Carl Reid.

Whatever happens next isn't going to be good, Trixie thought glumly. She didn't feel like facing the others, knowing that her sleuthing had put them all in the most horrible danger. *I should have taken everyone's advice for once and kept my nose out of this!*

One fact was now inescapable: Now there was no way to save themselves.

13 * The Rescuers

JUST WHEN Trixie thought her heart would break from guilt and despair, she heard a scraping sound outside the shop. Before she knew what was happening, the door was thrown open and Sergeant Molinson burst into the room.

Behind him came two of his men. All three held drawn guns. A quick look of shock passed over their faces as they took in the scene before them—the whole Bob-White group sitting tied up on the floor, and a table piled with money in the center of the room.

It was almost more than they could accept.

Sergeant Molinson quickly assessed the situation. As the three men in the back room spun around, reaching for their guns, the Sergeant was ready for them. Holding his gun in front of his face with both hands, he went into a partial crouch.

"Lay down the guns!" he snapped. "You're under arrest!"

The counterfeiters placed their heavy revolvers on the floor, and the Bob-Whites heaved a collective sigh of relief. The officers with Sergeant Molinson quickly went into the back room, and slapped handcuffs on the three men.

Trixie and Mart—not to mention the rest of the Bob-Whites—wanted to be untied instantly. But only after the Sergeant was completely satisfied that the alleged perpetrators were safely under lock and key did the police turn their attention to the Bob-Whites and Inspector Patou. Then with remarkable speed, they had them all untied and standing, happily rubbing their sore wrists and flexing their stiff arms. Trixie looked around her in wonder. Two minutes ago, she'd been convinced it was all over, and now, suddenly, they were safe and sound—and all thanks to Sergeant Molinson.

"Oh, wow," she said, turning to face him, a big grin on her face. "I've never been so glad to see anyone in my entire life! How did you know you were supposed to come and save us?"

"Well, I'm glad to hear you finally admit it, young lady," Sergeant Molinson said. There was a self-congratulatory smile on his face. "I saved you this time, and don't you ever forget it! I've had this operation under investigation for a long time. This time, I solved the crime for you, Miss Trixie Belden."

"This is true?" Marcel asked, stepping out from behind the rest of the Bob-Whites. "I, too, have had this operation under investigation."

"Who in tarnation is that?" Sergeant Molinson asked, focusing on the Inspector. It was obvious that, in the heat of the moment, he'd missed the large man completely.

"Oh, Sergeant Molinson," Trixie volunteered smugly. "This is Inspector Marcel Patou of the Paris Sûreté—that's police— special investigations—in case you didn't know. Anyway, he's been following us—I mean, he's been following these counterfeiters for ages, all the way from Paris and everything. He was helping us—I mean, actually, we were helping him catch the counterfeiters."

Trixie had to stop to catch her breath and organize her thoughts. As often happened when she was overexcited, her mouth got going faster than her brain and she got a little mixed up. But she had a good excuse, considering all she'd been through in the last three hours! Before she was able to finish her explanation, however, the Inspector began to speak for himself.

"Sergeant Molinson," he said, extending his hand. "I am very pleased to make your acquaintance. If you wish, I have here the identification."

Sergeant Molinson carefully scrutinized the papers, then handed them back.

"Yes," he continued as Sergeant Molinson stared thoughtfully at him. "I have been on this case for a year. But truly, it all began in Paris many, many years ago. You see, in 1824 Joseph Niepce, the partner of Louis Daguerre, made the first metal engraving by photography. So, you see, it is an obvious conclusion that the highest quality plates should come from Paris. Unfortunately, high quality plates can be used for many things—not all of them legal."

He stopped briefly and directed a baleful glare in the direction of the three men. None of them returned his gaze.

"There is in Paris a little shop which is the conduit for these particular illegal plates. They make engravings of currencies of all nations. I had the good fortune to be assigned to watch comings and goings on the day when these two young ladies came into the store." He gestured briefly at Trixie and Honey. While Sergeant Molinson looked at them in surprise, the Inspector continued. "I followed them all the way from Paris, and they led me right to these men."

"That's right, Sergeant Molinson," Trixie managed to get in. "But we didn't know that you were also investigating. What led you to be suspicious of The Antique Barn?"

Sergeant Molinson was annoyed at her question. "I don't have to divulge my sources to a kid," he snapped. "And furthermore . . ."

But just as he began to shake a warning finger at Trixie, the door of the shop burst open once again.

"Well, thank goodness," said a distraught Mrs. De Keyser, as she stomped into the room. She was dressed in a fuzzy blue bathrobe, her hair hanging loose down her back. She brandished a crowbar in her good hand. "It's about time you boys showed up! I called you a good hour ago!"

Trixie gasped, and Sergeant Molinson's face turned beet-red.

"It was a burglary, right?" Mrs. De Keyser continued. "I knew it! All those people sneaking around in the bushes! What in heaven's name took you so long?"

"Actually," Mart said, "he was right on time. The movie let out about five minutes ago."

"The movie?" Mrs. De Keyser asked. "What movie?"

"Oh, Mrs. De Keyser," Trixie said. "That's just my brother Mart. Pay no attention to him. It's a private joke."

"Oh, I know Mart," Mrs. De Keyser said. "And I know these other two nice young men as well." She looked around the room in bewilderment. "But what on earth are all you children doing here? And why have you put handcuffs on poor Mr. Reid? Sergeant Molinson, I assure you that Mr. Reid would hardly burglarize his own shop. Really!"

"Sorry ma'am," Sergeant Molinson said, "but I'm afraid that what was going on in here wasn't exactly a burglary. Unfortunately, I think you're going to have to find a new tenant. This Mr. Reid here happened to be part of a counterfeiting scam. They were in there printing up nice new phony twenties. See?"

He held a bundle of the offending articles up for Mrs. De Keyser to see. She gasped, and promptly dropped the crowbar. It landed with a resounding clang, and the noise made everyone jump.

"Heavenly days!" she said. "That means I'm an accomplice! After all, it was happening on my property, wasn't it?"

"Don't worry, ma'am," Sergeant Molinson said kindly. "You are in no way implicated. Now we have some work to do, if you'll excuse us."

"If you don't mind, Sergeant," the Inspector said, "I believe I should accompany you while you do the paper work. This group is wanted internationally as well. They might be inclined to name some of their accomplices on the other side of the Atlantic."

"Right," Sergeant Molinson said. "And you kids better get on home. Isn't it past your bedtime?"

"Don't you need us to testify or make a deposition?" Trixie asked hopefully. "I mean, we're all witnesses. And we were the ones who figured it out in the first place."

"That's right, officer," Honey said cheerfully. "We found the printing plates inside the doll's dress—you know, the doll we picked up for Mr. Reid in Paris—and that's when Trixie decided to stake out the store and catch Mr. Reid in the act of committing the crime."

"I see," Sergeant Molinson said. "Well, Inspector Patou here can fill me in on everything. If we need you, we'll call you. Now you should be getting on home, kids. It's late."

"He's right, Trixie," Brian said calmly. "Our time's about up. That movie let out a little while ago, and we still have to walk back home."

"Couldn't we say we stopped for hamburgers?" Mart asked hopefully.

"We could *say* anything we wanted," Di said, giggling. "But that wouldn't get us to Wimpy's."

"She's right, Mart," Dan said. "No wheels, no Wimpy's."

"Are you hungry, you poor things?" Mrs. De Keyser said. "After what you've accomplished this evening, you certainly deserve a snack."

"But Mrs. De Keyser—" Trixie said.

"No buts about it, young lady," the older woman interrupted. "I want you all to come over right this minute. I'll fix you some nice hot chocolate. And it just so happens that a neighbor brought me a dozen blueberry buns this afternoon. That's more than I can eat myself."

"Here, here!" Mart said happily. "And pay no attention to my sister, ma'am. She doesn't have the same needs that I have!"

The Bob-Whites watched solemnly as Carl Reid and his accomplices were handed into the police cars. Inspector Patou got in with Sergeant Molinson, and the little cavalcade wound onto Glen Road and headed for town.

Mrs. De Keyser led the Bob-Whites into her big kitchen to a chorus of hysterical barking from Willy. She listened to the whole story as she bustled around like a mother hen. With Honey and Trixie's help, she prepared hot chocolate and heated up blueberry buns in her oven.

The long story they told was punctuated with her little gasps of dismay and expressions of surprise.

Feeling a good deal warmer, and with pleasantly full stomachs, the weary Bob-Whites set out for their respective houses.

Mart, Brian, and Trixie said good-night to Dan and Di at the foot of the driveway to the Lynch estate. Dan was going to walk Di home before continuing on to the cabin he shared with Mr. Maypenny. Then Honey and Jim went up the driveway to the Manor House.

"Well, Trixie," said Mart as they trudged up the driveway to Crabapple Farm. "You and your sleuthing almost got us polished off this time. Think perhaps you'd consider retiring early?"

"Not a chance, Mart, ol' buddy," Trixie chortled. "If it hadn't been for me, you never would have gotten an opportunity to sample those blueberry buns. Stick with me, kid, and I'll show you all the good things in life!"

"If I live long enough," came his snappy reply.

The three contented Bob-Whites let themselves into the house as quietly as possible. But, to their surprise, Helen Belden and her husband were sitting up in the living room, watching the dancing flames in the fireplace.

"How was the movie?" Mrs. Belden asked sleepily.

"Very exciting," Trixie answered. "Actually, I can't tell you how exciting it was!"

"How lovely, dear," her mother replied fondly. "I'm so glad you all had such a nice time."

"Well, I don't know about nice," said Trixie with a pixyish smile, "but it *was* exciting!"

Then she climbed the stairs to her room, with a smile on her face.

14 * The Sergeant's Commendation

IN THE SEVERAL WEEKS since The Antique Barn closed its doors for good, Thanksgiving had come and gone. The Bob-Whites were now busy getting ready for Christmas. With the help of Dan Mangan, Brian had installed a small wood-burning stove in the clubhouse. It had been given to them by Mrs. De Keyser. She had found it in her cellar shortly after the incident in the shop.

"Oh, I really have no need of it now," she'd said. "It was used in the days before central heating was installed in the house."

Now, thanks to Mrs. De Keyser, they could meet in their clubhouse during the winter, and it was a good thing, too. It made a perfect place to work on their Christmas gifts—at least the ones that weren't for other Bob-Whites.

Mart was building a large wooden dump truck for Bobby, and he'd also sent away for plans on how to build a giant wooden salad bowl. It was two feet in diameter, and he was planning to present it to his mother—providing he could figure out the directions. They had turned out to be a lot more complicated than he'd expected.

Trixie, who hadn't arrived at the clubhouse yet, was knitting long, brightly colored scarfs for everyone she could think of. She had so much knitting to do as a result that she was certain her fingers would drop off.

Honey had decided to sew silk neckties for all the men and boys, and make sachets for the women with rose-petal potpourri. Carefully choosing rose petals after the morning dew had been dried by the sun, she had mixed them with special essences and oils. Then they had been set aside to get stronger. Now she was sewing little satin cases which she was planning to stuff with the scented, dried flowers.

Dan was whittling small wooden figures; Jim was binding together blank pages to make personal diaries; and Di was making Christmas decorations to give as gifts. She had already dipped walnuts and pinecones in gold paint, and was now covering Styrofoam balls with multicolored, embroidered ribbons.

It was cozy and warm in the clubhouse, and an air of busy productivity added to the comfortable hominess of the room.

"What time is it?" Di asked, as she tried to unstick her glue-covered fingers from the embroidered ribbon without pulling it off the Styrofoam ball.

"Seven-thirty," Brian answered. "Do you have to be home at any particular time?"

"Oh. Eleven at the latest," said Di. She finally managed to get herself unstuck. With a satisfied expression, she placed the ball on a sheet of clean paper to dry. "That wasn't why I asked. I was just wondering where Trixie is."

No sooner were the words out of her

mouth than the door burst open. A blast of chilly air and one Trixie Belden came into the room.

"Back to the salt mines," Trixie said cheerfully. She took off her hat, and shook out her short hair.

"Where have you been?" Mart asked.

"Well, basketball practice was a little late," she said, "but that wasn't all of it. Wait until you hear what I have to say! Carl Reid is facing a twenty-year sentence in the United States, and his accomplices in Europe have all been caught!"

"When did you hear that!" Mart exclaimed, sitting bolt upright. "How come nobody ever tells me these things!"

"Well, I saw Sergeant Molinson on my way home today," Trixie answered, trying to hide the smile that was tugging at the corners of her mouth. "He specifically asked me to let all of you know. Not only was Carl Reid a very big wheel in this particular ring, but his arrest led to the conviction of several other big criminals the government has been trying to pin something on for years. He especially told me to thank you all for your part in solving the mystery."

"Our part?" Brian said. "What does he mean by our part? It was you and Honey who did it all, practically single-handedly!"

"Now don't exaggerate!" Trixie said in her most humble tone. "Not quite."

"She's right, Brian." Mart said. "After all, I was there too, and that night I not only never got a hamburger, I almost was a hamburger!"

"And how about Inspector Patou?" Di asked. "Did Sergeant Molinson tell you anything about him?"

"Yes, as a matter of fact he did," Trixie answered. "He said that the Inspector was given a citation and a medal by the French government for closing down the European end of the operation."

"Not bad, not bad," Dan said with a smile.

"And Sergeant Molinson also gave me the reason Carl Reid asked Honey and me to pick up the plates. Mr. Reid knew the operation was being watched on the French end because his regular courier had been arrested. The idea of the antique doll came to him when he overheard us talking about our trip. After getting us to agree to do the dirty work, he quickly telephoned his French connection and instructed him to run out and

buy an antique doll—any antique doll—and
put the plates inside."

"Well, that certainly answers one question, doesn't it?" said Honey.

"Which one is that?" Brian asked.

"For the life of me, I couldn't figure out
why he asked us to go pick up the doll with
the plates, when it would have been so
much easier to simply mail the plates to a
box number or have one of his cronies pick
them up."

"Actually," Jim said, "it was a pretty smart
plan. He knew the French plate-makers
were being watched by the French police. If
they'd mailed them—or gotten a new courier—the French police could have notified
the American police who would then watch
the address, or the post office, or the airport
until someone came to pick up the plates.
That person would have led them straight to
Carl Reid."

"But instead, Mr. Reid planned it very
well," Mart said. "He sent two obviously
touristy American girls who were traveling
in a private jet instead of a scheduled airline.
That would make it almost impossible for a
French agent to track them down and trace

them back to him. He also knew that people traveling on private jets always breeze through customs."

"There was only one thing he didn't count on," Di said, with a laugh. "Carl Reid didn't understand what happens when you send Trixie to do anything!"

"It was his first mistake," Mart said in a theatrically deep voice, "and also his last!"

"And Sergeant Molinson said to tell you that without our nosy intervention," Trixie said, "Carl Reid would actually have gotten away with it."

"So the Sergeant admitted it, did he?" Mart said thoughtfully. "I never thought I'd see the day."

"Me either," Brian said. "Did he also say, 'And even though you're nosy, you'd be welcome on my force any day'?"

"Well, not in those exact words," Trixie said with a twinkle in her eye, "but it was close—and from Sergeant Molinson, that means a lot!"

"So, tell me," asked Dan. "What's Mrs. De Keyser going to do about that barn?"

"She found another tenant," Honey said.

"Really?" Brian said. "Who?"

"Well," Trixie answered, "it's going to be a crafts store next. And it looks like it'll be really nice, too."

"Oh, boy," Mart said sarcastically. "Just what we need around here—more knitting and crocheting! More darning needles and wool samplers. Well, you can bet there isn't anything very mysterious about a crafts store."

"I wouldn't be too sure about that," Trixie chided. Then she laughed. "After all, what could possibly have been crooked about an antique store?"